Freeland
A Social Anticipation
Book IV

By

Theodor Hertzka

ABOUT THE AUTHOR

Theodor Hertzka, sometimes known as Hertzka Tivadar, was an economist and journalist of Jewish, Hungarian, and Austrian heritage. He studied at Vienna and Budapest universities before joining the editorial team of Vienna's Neue Freie Presse in 1872. He started the journal Wiener Allgemeine Zeitung in 1879 and served as its editor until 1886. He was friends with Johannes Brahms. Hertzka has been dubbed the "Austrian Bellamy" since his work Freiland, ein soziales Zukunftsbild shares a subject with Edward Bellamy's novel Looking Backward. Though Hertzka was not a Zionist, and his utopian vision was aimed toward humans in general, Theodor Herzl acknowledged Hertzka's impact on his own views in the first chapter of his book Der Judenstaat, which envisaged the establishment of a Jewish state.

CONTENTS

CHAPTER XXIII

The moral effect of our Abyssinian campaign was immense among all the civilised and half-civilised peoples who heard of it. We ourselves had expected the most salutary results from it, as we foresaw that the brilliant proof of our power which we had given to the world would make our adversaries more cautious and induce them to be more compliant to our just wishes. But the effect far exceeded our most sanguine expectations. The former opponents of economic justice were not merely silenced, but actually converted--a fact which seemed to astonish us Freelanders ourselves rather than our friends abroad. We could not clearly understand why people, who for decades had regarded our efforts as foolish or objectionable, should, simply because our young men had shown themselves to be excellent soldiers, suddenly conclude that it would be possible and beneficial to enable every worker to retain the full produce of his industry. The connection between the latter and the execution done by our rifles and cannons was not clear to us who lived under the dominion of reason and justice; but outside of Freeland, wherever physical force was still the ultimate ground of right, everybody--even those who in principle endorsed our ideas--held it to be a matter of course that the crushing blows under whose tremendous force the Negus of Abyssinia fell, were an unanswerable *argumentum ad hominem* for the superiority of our institutions as a whole. In particular, the sudden victorious appearance of our fleet operated abroad as a decisive proof that economic justice is no mere dream-Utopia, but a very real actuality; in short, our military successes proved to be the triumph of our social institutions. A strong feverish excitement took possession of all minds; and men everywhere now wished practically to adopt what until then had been seriously regarded by a comparatively small number as an ideal to be attained in the future, by many had been treated with disfavour, and by most had been altogether ignored.

And it was seen--which certainly did *not* surprise us--that the impatience and the revolutionary fever were the intenser the less the subjects of them had previously studied our principles. The most advanced liberal-minded nations, whose foremost statesmen had already been in sympathy with us, and had made well-meant, but disconnected, attempts to lead their working-classes into industrial freedom, applied themselves with comparative deliberateness to the task of effecting the great economic and social revolution with as little disturbance of the existing interests as possible. England, France, and Italy, which before the outbreak of the Abyssinian war were already prepared to introduce our institutions into their East African possessions, now resolved to co-operate with us in the conversion of their existing institutions into others analogous to ours--a course which they could take without involving themselves in any very revolutionary steps. Several other European Powers, as well as the whole of America and Australia, immediately followed their example. This gave rise to some stormy outbursts of popular feeling in the States in question; but beyond the breaking of a few windows no harm was done. There were more serious disturbances in the 'conservative' States of Europe and in some parts of Asia; there occurred violent uprisings and serious attacks upon unpopular ministers, who in vain asserted that they no longer had any objection to make to economic equity. Here and there the struggle led to bloodshed and confiscations. The working-classes mistrusted the wealthy classes, but were themselves not agreed upon the course that should be taken; and the parties assumed a more and more threatening attitude towards each other. But the condition of affairs was worst where the governments had formerly acted in avowed opposition to the people, the wealthy had oppressed the masses, and the latter had been designedly kept in ignorance and poverty. In such countries there was no intelligent popular class possessing influence enough to control the outbursts of furious and unreasoning hatred; cruelty and horrors of all kinds were perpetrated, the former oppressors slaughtered wholesale, and there would have been no means of staying the senseless and aimless bloodshed if, fortunately for these countries, our influence and authority had not ultimately quieted the raging masses and turned the agitation into proper channels. After one of the parties, which in those countries were fruitlessly tearing each other to pieces, had conceived the idea of calling in our intervention, the example was generally followed. Wherever anarchy prevailed in the east of Europe, in Asia, in several African States, requests were sent that we would furnish commissioners, to whom should be granted unlimited authority. We naturally complied most gladly with these requests; and the Freeland commissioners were everywhere the objects of that implicit confidence which was necessary for the restoration of quiet.

In the meantime those States also which were more advanced in opinion had asked for confidential agents from Freeland to assist, both with counsel and material aid, the governments in prosecuting the intended reforms. We say advisedly with counsel and *material aid* for the people of Freeland, as soon as it was known that assistance had been asked for, granted to their delegates, whether acting as consultative members of a foreign government or as commissioners furnished with unlimited power, disposal over the material resources of Freeland for the benefit of the countries that had sent for them; the sums advanced being treated not as gifts, but as loans. The central government of Eden Vale formally reserved the right to give the final decision in the case of each loan; but as it was an understood principle that necessary help was to be afforded, and as only those who were on the spot could know what help was necessary, a discretionary right of disposal of the available capital really lay in the hands of the commissioners and confidential agents.

That we were able, in the course of a few months, to meet a demand from abroad for nearly two milliard pounds sterling is explained by the fact that our Freeland Insurance Department had at its disposal in an available form about one-fifth of its reserve of more than ten milliards sterling. The other four-fifths were invested--that is, it was lent to associations and to the commonwealth for various purposes; the one-fifth had been retained in the coffers of the bank as disposable stock for emergencies, and now could be used to meet the sudden demand for capital. This reserve, of course, was not kept in the form of gold or silver: had it been, it would not have been available when an accidental demand arose. It is not gold or silver, but quite other things that are required in a time of need: the precious metals can serve merely as suitable means of procuring the things that are really required. In order that such things may be acquired they must exist somewhere in a sufficient quantity, and that they exist in sufficient quantity to meet a sudden and exceptionally large demand cannot be taken for granted. He who suddenly wants goods worth milliards of pounds will not be able to buy them anywhere, because they are nowhere stored up to that amount; if he would be protected from the danger of not being able to get such a demand met, he must lay up, not the money for purchase, but the goods themselves which he expects to need. Take, for example, the case of the Russians who had burnt and destroyed the granaries of their landowners, the warehouses of their merchants, the machines in their factories: what good would have done them had the milliards of roubles which they needed to make good--and to add to--what had been destroyed been sent to them in the form of money for them to spend? There were no surplus supplies which they could have bought: had they taken our money into the markets the only effect would have been to raise all prices, and to have made all the neighbouring nations share their distress. And in the same way all the other nations, which we wished to assist in their endeavour to rise as quickly as possible out of their misery into a state of wealth similar to our own, needed not increased currency but increased food, raw material, and implements. And our reserve was laid up in the form of such things.

About half of it always consisted of grain, the other half of various kinds of raw material, particularly materials for weaving, and metals. When our commissioner in Russia asked at different times for sums amounting altogether to £285,000,000, he did not receive from us a farthing in money, but 3,040 cargoes of wheat, wool, iron, copper, timber, &c.: the result was that the wasted country did not suffer at all from want, but a few months later--certainly less in consequence of the loans themselves than of the fact that the loans were employed in the Freeland spirit--it enjoyed a prosperity which a short time before no one would have dreamt to be possible. In the same way we made our resources useful to other nations, and we resolved that should our existing means not suffice to meet the demands, we would make up what was still needed from the produce of the coming year.

We by no means intended to continue this *rôle* of economic and social providence to our brother peoples longer than was absolutely necessary. We did not shrink from either the burden or the responsibility; but we considered that in all respects it would be for the best if the process of social reconstruction, in which all mankind was now engaged, were to be carried out with the united powers of all, according to a well-considered common plan. We therefore determined at once to invite all the nations of the earth to a conference at Eden Vale, in which it might be decided what ought next to be done. It was not our intention that this congress should pass binding resolutions: it should remain, we thought, free to every nation to draw what conclusions it pleased from the discussions at the congress; but it seemed to us that in any case it would be of advantage to know what the majority thought of the movement now going on.

This suggestion met with no serious objection anywhere. Among the less advanced nations of Asia there was a strong feeling that, instead of spending the time in useless talk, it would be better simply to put into execution whatever we Freelanders advised. The constituent assemblies of several--and those not the least--nations said that they on their part would abide by what we said, whatever the congress might decide upon. But it was necessary only to point out that we could not advise them until we had heard them, and that a congress seemed to be the best means of making their wants known, to induce them to send delegates. We could not prevent many of the delegates from receiving instruction to vote with us Freelanders in all divisions whatever--an instruction which proved to be quite unnecessary, as the congress did not divide at all, except upon questions of form, upon other questions confining itself to discussion and leaving everyone to draw his own conclusions from the debates.

On the other hand, in the most advanced countries a small minority had organised an opposition, not, it is true, against the general principles of economic justice, but against many of the details involved in carrying out that principle. This opposition had nowhere been able to elect a delegate who should bear its mandate to the World's Congress; but it everywhere found strong advocates among the Freeland confidential agents and commissioners, who, while perfectly in harmony with the public opinion of Freeland, endeavoured, as far as possible, to secure a representation of every considerable party tendency, in order that those who clung to the obsolete old economic order should have no right to complain that they could not make themselves heard. Sixty-eight nations were invited to take part in the congress; it was left to the nations themselves to decide how many delegates they should send, provided they did not send more than ten each. The sixty-eight countries elected 425 delegates, thus making with the twelve heads of departments of the Freeland government a total number of 437 members of the congress.

On the 3rd of March, in the twenty-sixth year after the founding of Freeland, the congress met in the large hall of the Eden Vale National Palace. On the right sat those who questioned the possibility of carrying out the proposed reform universally, in the centre the adherents of Freeland, on the left the Radicals to whom the most violent measures seemed best. The presidency was given to the head of the Freeland government, which position had been uninterruptedly occupied by Dr. Strahl since the founding of the commonwealth.

We give the following *résumé* of the six days' discussion from the official minutes:

First Day

The President, in the name of the Freeland people, welcomed the delegates of the nations who had responded to the Freeland invitation.

Charles Montaigne (*Centre*), in the name of his colleagues, thanked the Freeland people for the magnanimous and extraordinary assistance which they had afforded to the other nations of the earth in their struggles after economic freedom. Not content with showing to the rest of the world the way to economic freedom and justice, Freeland had also made enormous material sacrifices. For his part, he did not know which was the more astonishing, the inexhaustibleness of the resources which Freeland had at its disposal or the disinterested magnanimity exhibited in the employment of those resources.

James Clark (*Freeland*): In the interest of sober truth, as well as with a view of furthering as much as possible the great work we all have at heart, I must explain that though the Freeland people are always happy to make disinterested sacrifices for the good of their brother peoples, and that in all they do in this way their object is rather to develop and to promote the best interests of mankind than to obtain any advantage for themselves, yet, as a matter of fact, the milliards lent to foreign countries cost Freeland no material sacrifice, but bring it considerable material profit. [Sensation.] Under the *régime* of economic justice and freedom the solidarity of all economic interests is so universal and without exception, that in Freeland business becomes as profitable as it is possible to conceive of its being while you, with our assistance, are growing rich most rapidly. This would be true if we gave you the milliards instead of lending them. You look at each other and at me with an inquiring astonishment? You hold it to be impossible to become rich by lending gratuitously or by absolutely giving away a part of one's property? Yet nothing is simpler. The subject is a very important one, and will come up for discussion again in the course of our sittings; at present I will only briefly point out that we have been prevented by the misery of the rest of the world from making the right use of the advantages of international division of labour. We have been obliged to manufacture for ourselves goods which we might have obtained better from you; and we have therefore had to produce a smaller quantity of those things which we could have produced most profitably. It is plain that we should be far richer if we could give our attention chiefly to the production of grain for ourselves and for you, and derive from you the supplies we need to meet our demand for manufactured articles. For here the soil yields for an equal amount of labour and capital ten times as much as among you, while few manufactures here yield a larger return for labour and capital than they do abroad. But, on account of the system of exploitation which has prevailed and is not yet got rid of among you--the cheap wages consequent upon which have cramped your use of labour-saving machinery--we have been, and still are, compelled to meet most of our demand for manufactured articles by our own production, since you are scarcely able to produce for yourselves, to say nothing of producing for us, a great number of goods which in the nature of things you ought to be able to produce most profitably both for yourselves and for us, and in exchange for which you would receive our foodstuffs and raw material. We calculate that the removal of this hindrance to the complete international division of labour must increase the productiveness of our labour so much that the resulting gain would be cheaply bought by a permanent sacrifice of many milliards. You need not wonder, then, at finding us always so eager in encouraging you to make the freest and fullest claims upon our resources. You will never dip so deeply into our pockets that we--in our own interest as well as in yours--will not wish to see you dip still deeper. Every farthing spent in hastening the development of your wealth is made good to us ten and twentyfold.

Francis Far (*Right*): If it is so much to the interest of Freeland to enrich us that Freeland is profited even by making us a gift of its capital, why has it not given us its capital sooner? Who would have hindered it from handing its milliards over to us? Why did it delay so long, and why does it now make its assistance conditional on our accepting its economic institutions?

James Clark: Because so long as you remained in servitude every farthing given to you for such a purpose would have been simply thrown away. Formerly we could do nothing more than support the victims of your social system and mitigate the misery and wretchedness you inflicted upon yourselves. As a matter of fact, there have long been large sums of Freeland capital--bearing interest, it is true--invested in Europe and America. What has been the result? This money has contributed to increase the amount of surplus capital among you: it could not increase the quantity of capital actually employed in production among you, for nothing could have done that but an increased consumption by the people outside of Freeland--and this was not compatible with what were then your economic principles. Therefore we have been able to help you only since you yourselves have held out the hand: our capital will benefit you only because you have at length decided to enjoy the fruits of it yourselves. [General assent.]

The President: In order to preserve a certain amount of order in our discussions, I propose that we at once agree upon a list of the questions to be considered. It may not always be possible to adhere strictly to the order in the list; but it is advisable that each speaker should endeavour as much as possible to confine himself to the subject under discussion. In order to expedite matters, the Freeland government has prepared a kind of agenda, which you can accept, or amend, or reject. The matters for discussion mentioned in this agenda, I may remark, were not introduced on our initiative, but were mentioned by the leaders of the different parties abroad as needing more detailed explanation: we, on our part, contented ourselves with arranging these questions. We propose, therefore, that the following be the order in which the subjects be discussed:

1. How can the fact be explained that never in the course of history, before the founding of Freeland, has there been a successful attempt to establish a commonwealth upon the principles of economic justice and freedom?

2. Is not the success of the Freeland institutions to be attributed merely to the accidental, and therefore probably transient, co-operation of specially favourable circumstances; or do those institutions rest upon conditions universally present and inherent in human nature?

3. Are not want and misery necessary conditions of existence; and would not over-population inevitably ensue were misery for a time to disappear from the earth?

4. Is it possible to introduce the institutions of economic justice everywhere without prejudice to inherited rights and vested interests; and, if possible, what are the best means of doing this?

5. Are economic justice and freedom the ultimate outcome of human evolution; and what will probably be the condition of mankind under such a *régime*?

Has anyone a remark to make upon our proposal? No one has. Therefore I place point 1 upon the order of the day, and call upon delegate Erasmus Kraft to speak.

Erasmus Kraft (*Right*): Wherever thinking men dwell upon this earth, we are preparing to exchange the state of servitude and misery in which from time immemorial our race has been sunk, for a happier order of things. The brilliant example which we have before our eyes here in Freeland seems to be a pledge that our attempt will--nay, must--succeed. But the more evident this certainty becomes, the more urgent, the more imperative, becomes the question why that which is now to be accomplished has not long since been done, why the genius of humanity slept so long before it roused itself to the task of completing this richly beneficent work. And the simpler--the more completely in harmony with human nature and with the most primitive requirements of sound reason--appears to be the complex of those institutions upon which the work of emancipation depends, so much the more enigmatical is it that earlier centuries and millenniums, when there was no lack of enlightened and noble minds, never seriously attempted to accomplish such a work. We see that it suffices to guarantee to everyone the full enjoyment of what he produces, in order to supply everyone with more than enough; and yet through untold millenniums men have patiently endured boundless misery with all its consequences of sorrow and crime as if they were inevitable conditions of existence. Why was this? Are we shrewder, wiser, juster than all our ancestors; or, in spite of all the apparently infallible evidence in favour of the success of our work, are we not perhaps under a delusion? It is true that the greatest and most important part of the history of mankind is veiled in the obscurity of primitive antiquity; yet history is so old that it is scarcely to be assumed that the endeavour after the material well-being of all--an endeavour prompted by the most ardent desires of every creature--should now make its appearance for the first time. It must be that such an endeavour has been put forth, not *once* merely but repeatedly, even though no tradition has given us any trustworthy account of it. But where are its results? Or did its results once exist though we know nothing of them? Is the story of the Golden Age something more than a pious fable; and are we upon the point of conjuring up another Golden Age? And then arises the query, how long will this Golden Age last; will it not again be followed by an age of bronze and an age of iron, perhaps in a more wretched, more humble form than that exhibited by the age from which we are preparing to part? Is that fatalistic resignation, with which the ages known to us endured misery and servitude, a human instinct evolved during an earlier and bitter experience--an instinct which teaches mankind to endure patiently the inevitable rather than strive after a brief epoch of happiness and progress at the risk of a deeper fall? In obedience to the hint from the chair, I will at present refrain from inquiring what might be the cause of such a relapse into redoubled misery, as this will be the theme of the third point in the list of subjects for discussion; but I think that before we proceed to an exposition of all the conceivable consequences of the success of our endeavours it would be advisable first to find out *whether* those endeavours will really and in their full extent succeed; and in order to find this out, it will again be advisable to ask why such endeavours have never succeeded before--nay, perhaps, why they have never before been made.

Christian Castor (*Centre*): The previous speaker is in error when he asserts that history tells us of no serious attempt to realise the principle of economic justice. One of the grandest attempts of this kind is Christianity. Everyone who knows the Gospels must know that Christ and His apostles condemned the exploitation of man by man. The words of Scripture, 'Woe to him who waxes fat upon the sweat of his brother,' contain *in nuce* the whole codex of Freeland law and all that we are now striving to realise. That the official Christianity afterwards allowed its work of emancipation to drop is true; but individual Fathers of the Church have again and again, in reliance upon the sacred text, endeavoured to realise the original purposes of Christ. And that during the Middle Ages, as well as in modern times, vigorous attempts to realise the Christian ideal--that is, the ideal of Christ, not that of the Church--have never been wanting is also well known. This is what I wished to point out. The elucidation of the question why all these attempts were wrecked I leave to other and better furnished minds.

Vladimir Ossip (*Left*): Far be it from me to hold the noble Founder of Christianity responsible for what was afterwards made out of His teaching; but our friend from the United States goes, in my opinion, too far when he represents Christ and His successors as *our* predecessors. We proclaim prosperity and freedom--Christ preached self-denial and humility; we desire the wealth, He the poverty, of all; we busy ourselves with the things of this world--He had the next world before His eyes; we are--to speak briefly--revolutionaries, though pacific ones--He is the founder of a religion. Let us leave religion alone; I do not think it will be of any use for us to call in question the *meum* and *tuum* as to Christianity.

Lionel Acosta (*Centre*): I differ entirely in this case from the previous speaker, and agree with our colleague from North America. The teaching of Christ, though not explicit as to means and ends, is the purest and noblest proclamation of social freedom that has yet been heard, and it is this proclamation of social emancipation, and not any religious novelty, that forms the substance of the 'Good News.' It was a master-stroke of the policy of enslavement to represent Christ as a founder of a religion instead of a social reformer: the latter doctrine had quickly won the hearts of the oppressed masses because it promised them release from their sufferings, but the former doctrine was used to lull to sleep their awakening energy.

Christ did not concern Himself with religion--not a line in the Gospels shows the slightest trace of His having interfered with one of the ancient religious precepts of His country. The most orthodox Jew can unhesitatingly place the Gospels in the hands of his children, certain that they will find nothing therein to wound their religious sentiment. [A Voice: Then why was Christ crucified?] I am asked why Christ was crucified if He had done nothing contrary to the Mosaic law. Do men commit murder from religious motives *merely*? Christ was hurried to death because He was a *social*, not because He was a religious, innovator; and it was not the pious but the powerful among the Jews who demanded His death. Scarcely a word is needed to set this matter right in the minds of all those who study without prejudice the momentous events of that saddest, but at the same time most glorious, of the days of Israel, upon which the noblest of her sons voluntarily sought and found a martyr's death. In the first place, it is a well-attested historical fact that in Judaea at that time death for religious heresy was as little known as in Europe during the last century. In the second place, the mode of execution--the cross, which was quite foreign to the Jews--shows that Christ was executed according to Roman, not Jewish, law. But the Romans, the most tolerant in religious matters of all peoples, would never have put a man to death for religious innovation; they would not have allowed the execution to take place, much less have themselves pronounced sentence and carried out that sentence in their own method. The cross was among them the punishment for *riotous slaves* or their *instigators*. I do not say this for the purpose of shifting the responsibility for Christ's death from Judaea--it is the sad privilege of that people to have been the executioner of its noblest sons; and as only the Athenians killed Socrates, so none but the Jews killed Christ; the Romans were only the instruments of Jewish hatred--the hatred, that is, of those wealthy men among the Jews of the time who denounced the 'perverter of the people' to the Governor because they trembled for their possessions. Indeed, it is quite credible that the Governor did not show himself willing to accede to the wishes of the eager denouncers, for he, the Roman, who had grown up in unshaken faith in the firmly established rights of property, did not understand the significance and bearing of the social teaching of Christ. The Gospels leave us little room to doubt--and it would be difficult to understand how it could be otherwise--that he held Christ to be a harmless enthusiast, who might have been let off with a little scourging. Generations had to pass away before the *Roman* world could learn what the teaching of Christ really was; and then it fell upon His followers with a fury without a parallel--crucified them, threw them to the beasts; in short, did everything that Rome was accustomed to do to the foes of its system of law and property, but never to the followers of foreign religions. It was different with the *Jewish* aristocracy: these at once understood the meaning and the bearing of the Christian propaganda, for they had long since learnt the germ of these social demands in the Pentateuch and in the teaching of the earlier prophets. The year of Jubilee which required a fresh division of the land after every forty-nine years, the regulation that all slaves should be emancipated in the seventh year--what were these but the precursors of the universal equality demanded by Christ? Whether all these ideas, which are to be found in the Sacred Scriptures of ancient Judaea, were ever realised in practice is more than doubtful. But they were currently known to every Jew; and when Christ attempted to give them a practical form--when, in vigorous and rousing addresses, He denounced woe to the rich man who fattened upon his brother's sweat--then the powerful in Jerusalem at once recognised that their interests were threatened by a danger which was not clearly seen by non-Jewish property-owners until much later. There is not the slightest doubt that they made no secret of the true grounds of their anxiety to the Roman Governor, for Christ was executed, not as a sectary, but as an inciter to revolt.

But, of course, it could not be told to the people that the death of Christ was demanded because He wished to put into practice the principle of equality laid down in the sacred books and so often insisted on by the prophets. The people had to be satisfied with the fable of the religious heresy of the Nazarene, which fable, however--except in the case of the unjudging crowd that collected together at the crucifixion--for a long time found no credence. Everywhere in Israel did the first Christian communities pass for good Jews; they were called *Judaei* by all the Roman authors by whom they were mentioned. What they really were, in what respects alone they differed from the other communities of Jews, is sufficiently revealed in the Acts of the Apostles, notwithstanding the very natural caution of the writer, and the subsequent equally intelligible corruptions of the text. They were Socialists, to some extent Communists; absolute economic equality, community of goods, was practised among them. Later, when the Christian Church sacrificed its social principle to peace with the State, and transformed itself from a cruelly persecuted martyr to equality into an instrument of authority and--perhaps because of this apostasy--of a doubly zealous persecuting authority, then first did she put forth as her own teaching the malicious calumny of her former maligners, and took upon herself the *rôle* of a new religion; and since then she has, in fact, been the propounder of a new religion. And that she has succeeded, for more than 1,500 years, in connecting her new *rôle* with the name of Christ, is mainly the fault of the Jews, who, through the sanguinary persecutions which have been carried on against them in the name of the meek Sufferer of Golgotha, have allowed themselves to be betrayed into a blind and foolish hatred towards this their greatest and noblest son.

But it remains none the less true that Christ suffered death for the idea of social justice and for this alone--nay, that before His time this idea was not unknown to Judaism. And it is equally true that notwithstanding all subsequent obscuration and corruption of this world-redeeming idea, the propaganda of economic emancipation has never since been completely suppressed. It was in vain that the Church forbad the laity to read those books which were alleged to contain no teaching but that of the Church: again and again did the European peoples, languishing in the deepest degradation, derive from those forbidden Scriptures courage and inspiration to attempt their emancipation.

Darja-Sing (*Centre*): I should like to add to what I have just heard that another people, six centuries before Christ, also conceived the ideas of freedom and justice--I mean the Indian people. The essence of Buddhism is the doctrine of the equality of all men and of the sinfulness of oppression and exploitation. Nay, I venture to assert that the already mentioned ideas of social freedom to be found in the Pentateuch, and held by the prophets, and consequently those also held by Christ, are to be referred back to Indian suggestion. At first sight this appears to be an anachronism, for Buddha lived six centuries before Christ, while the Jewish legends carry back the composition of the Pentateuch to the fourteenth century before Christ. But recent investigations have almost certainly established that these alleged books of Moses were composed in the sixth century B.C. at the earliest-- at any rate, after the return of the Israelites from the so-called Babylonish captivity. Now, just at the time when the *élite* of the then existing Jews were carried to Babylon, Buddha sent his apostles through the whole of Asia; and it may safely be assumed that those who 'wept by the waters of Babylon' were specially susceptible to the teaching of such apostles.

When, therefore, certain eminent German thinkers assert that Christianity is a drop of foreign blood in the Arian peoples, they are certainly correct in so far as Christianity actually came to them as Semitism, as having sprung from Judaism; nevertheless the Arian world can lay claim to the fundamental conception of Christianity as its own, since it is most highly probable that the Semitic peoples received the first germ of it from the Arians. I say this not for the purpose of depreciating the service performed by the great Semitic martyr to freedom. I cannot, alas! deny that we Arians were not able to accomplish anything of our own strength with the divine idea that sprang from our bosom. While it is probable that the horrors of the Indian system of caste, that most shameful blossom that ever sprang from the blood-and-tear-bedewed soil of bondage, made India the scene of the first intellectual reaction against this scourge of mankind, it is certain, on the other hand, that that very system of caste so severely strained the energy of our Indian people as to make it impossible for them to give practical effect to the reaction. Buddhism was extinguished in India, and outside of India it was soon entirely robbed of its social characteristic. Those transcendental speculations to which even in the West it was *attempted* to limit Christianity have in Eastern Asia been in reality the only effects of Buddhism. Indeed, the idea of freedom took different forms in the minds of the founders--taking one form in the Indian Avatar which, notwithstanding all his sublimity, bore the mark of his nationality; and taking another form in the Messiah of Judah who saw the light of the world in the midst of a people fired with a never-subdued yearning for freedom. Buddha could conceive of freedom only in the form of that hopeless self-renunciation which was falsely introduced into the Christian idea of freedom by those who did not wish to have their own enjoyments interfered with by the claims of others.

In fact, I am convinced that even our more vigorous kinsmen who had migrated to the West could not have given practical effect to the conception of freedom and equality if we--the Indian world--had transmitted to them that conception just as we had conceived it. For even those who migrated westward carried in their blood to Europe, and retained for a thousand years, the sentiment of caste. The idea that all men are equal, really equal here upon earth, would have remained as much beyond the grasp of the German noble and the German serf as it has remained beyond the grasp of the Indian Pariah or Sudra and the Brahman or Kshatriya. This conception had first to be condensed and permanently fixed by the genius of the strongly democratic little Semitic race on the banks of the Jordan, and then to be subjected to a severe--and, for a time, adverse--analytical criticism by the independent and logical spirit of research of Rome and Greece, before it could be transplanted and bear fruit in purely Arian races. It is very evident that the converted German kings adopted Christianity because they held it to be a convenient instrument of power. It was for the time being immaterial to them what the new doctrine had to say to the serfs; for the serf who looked up to the 'offspring of the gods,' his master, with awful reverence, seemed to be for ever harmless, and the only persons against whom it was necessary for the masters to arm were their fellow lords, the great and the noble, who differed from the kings in nothing but in the amount of their power. The right to rule came, according to the Arian view, from God: very well, but the right of the least of the nobles sprang, like that of the king, from the gods. Now, the kings found in Christ the *one* supreme Lord who had conferred power upon them, and upon them alone. They alone now possessed a divine source of authority; and therefore history shows us everywhere that it was the kings who introduced Christianity against the--often determined--opposition of the great, and never that the great were converted without, or against the will of, the kings. The masses of the people, the serfs, where were these ever asked? They have to do and believe what their masters think well; and without exception they do it, making no resistance whatever--allowing themselves to be driven to baptism in flocks like sheep, and believing, as they are commanded to do, that all power comes from *one* God, who bestows it upon *one* lord. For the Arian serf is a mere chattel without a will, and will not think for himself until he is educated to do so. This work of education has been a long time in progress; but, as the previous speaker rightly said, the idea of freedom has never slept.

Erich Holm (*Right*): I do not think that any valid objection can be made to the statement that the general idea of economic justice is thousands of years old and has never been completely lost sight of. But it is a question whether this general idea of equality of rights and of freedom has much in common with that which *we* are now about to put into practice, or whether in many respects it does not differ from that ancient idea. And, further, it is a question whether that idea, which we have heard is already twenty-five centuries old, has ever been or can be realised.

With reference to the first question, I must admit that Christ, in contrast to Buddha, entertained not a transcendental and metaphysical, but a very material and literal idea of equality. It is true that He pronounced the poor in spirit blessed; but the rich, who according to Him would find it harder to get into heaven than it is for a rope of camel's hair to go through a needle's eye, were not the rich in spirit, but the rich in earthly riches. It is also true that he said, 'My kingdom is not of this world' and 'Render unto Caesar the things that are Caesar's'; yet everyone who reads these passages in connection with their context must see that He is simply waiving all interference whatever with political affairs--that in wishing to gain the victory for social justice he is influenced not by political, but by transcendental aims for the sake of eternal blessedness. Whether Rome or Israel rules is immaterial to Him, if only justice be exercised; yet only pious narrow-mindedness can deny that He wished to see justice exercised here below, and not merely in the next world. But is that which Christ understands by justice really identical with what we mean by it? It is true that the 'Love thy neighbour as thyself,' which He preached in common with other Jewish teachers, would be a senseless phrase if it did not imply economic equality of rights. The man who exploits man loves man as he does his domestic animal, but not as himself: to require true 'Christian neighbourly love' in an exploiting society would be simply absurd, and what would come of it we have in times past sufficiently experienced. Indeed, the apostle removes all doubt from this point, for he expressly condemns the getting rich upon another's sweat.

So far, then, we are completely at one with Christ. But He just as emphatically condemns wealth and praises poverty, whilst we would make wealth the common possession of all, and therefore would place all our fellow-men in a condition in which--to speak with Christ--it would be harder to enter the kingdom of heaven than it is for a rope to go through a needle's eye. Here is a contradiction which it seems to me can scarcely be reconciled. We hold misery, Christ held wealth, to be the source of vice, of sin: our equality is that of wealth, His that of poverty. This is my first point.

In the second place, Christ did *not* succeed, modest as His aims were. Is not, then, an appeal to this noblest of all minds calculated to discourage rather than to encourage us in the pursuit of our aims?

Emilio Lerma (*Freeland*): The previous speaker has brought the poverty which Christ praised and required into a false relation with the--alleged-- miscarriage of His work of emancipation. Christ's work miscarried not in spite of, but *because* of, the fact that He attempted to base equality upon poverty. The equality of poverty cannot be established, for it would be synonymous with the stagnation of civilisation. However, it is not only possible, but necessary, to bring about the equality of wealth, as soon as the necessary conditions exist, because this is synonymous with the progress of civilisation. You will say that certainly this is so according to our view; but according to the view of Christ wealth is an evil. Very true. But when we examine the matter without prejudice, it is impossible not to see *that Christ rejected wealth only because it had its source in exploitation.* There is nothing in the life of Christ to suggest that He was such a gloomy ascetic as He must have been if He had held wealth, as such, to be sinful: numberless passages in the Gospels afford unequivocal evidence of the contrary. Christ's daily needs were very simple, but He was always ready to enjoy whatever His adherents offered him, and never saw any harm in getting as much pleasure from living as was consistent with justice. This view of His was not affected even by the hatred with which the rich of Jerusalem persecuted Him, and the often-quoted condemnation of the rich has in it something contrary to the spirit of the Gospels, if we tear it away from its connection with the words, 'Woe unto him who waxeth fat upon the sweat of his brother.' In condemning wealth, Christ condemned merely its source; the kingdom of heaven was closed to wealth because, and only because, wealth could not be acquired except by exploiting the sweat of men. There can be no doubt that Christ, like ourselves, would have become reconciled to wealth if then, as in our days, wealth were possible without exploitation--nay, really possible only without it. We shall have further occasion to discuss why this was impossible in Christ's day and for many centuries afterwards; at present it is enough to know that it *was* impossible, that the only choice lay between poverty and wealth with exploitation.

Christ rendered the immortal service of having recognised this alternative more clearly than anyone before Him, and of having attacked exploitation with soul-stirring fervour. It was inevitable that He should be crucified for what He did, for in the antagonism between justice and the claims of civilisation the first always succumbs. It was inevitable that He should die, because He unrolled the banner of true human love, freedom, and equality--in short, of all the noblest sentiments of the human heart-- nearly two thousand years too soon; too soon, that is, for Him, not for us: for dull-witted humanity needed those two thousand years in order fully to understand what its martyr meant. For humanity Christ died not a day too soon. There is, then, no contradiction between the Christian ideas and what we are striving for; the difference between the two lies simply herein: that the first announcement of the idea of equality was made in an age when the material conditions necessary for the practical realisation of this divine idea did not yet exist, whilst our endeavours signify the 'Incarnation of the Word,' the fruit of the seed then cast into the mind of mankind. It cannot, therefore, be said that the Christian work of emancipation has really 'miscarried': there merely lie two thousand years between the beginning and the completion of the work undertaken by Christ.

On account of the lateness of the hour the President here closed the sitting, the debate standing adjourned until the next day.

CHAPTER XXIV

Second Day

(Adjourned Discussion upon the first point on the Agenda)

Leopold Stockau (*Centre*) re-opened the debate: I think that the preliminary question, whether our present endeavours after economic justice really are without any historical precedent, was exhaustively discussed yesterday and was answered in the negative. At least, I am authorised by yesterday's speakers of the opposite party to declare that they are fully convinced that the teaching of Christ differs in no essential point from that which is practically carried out in Freeland, and which we wish to make the common property of the whole world. We now come to the main subject of the first question for discussion--namely, to the inquiry why the former attempts to base human industry upon justice and freedom have been unsuccessful.

The answer to this question has already been suggested by the last speaker of yesterday. Former attempts miscarried because they aimed at establishing the equality of poverty: ours will succeed because it implies the equality of wealth. The equality of poverty would have produced stagnation in civilisation. Art and science, the two vehicles of progress, assume abundance and leisure; they cannot exist, much less can they develop, if there are no persons who possess more than is sufficient to satisfy their merely animal wants. In former epochs of human culture it was impossible to create abundance and leisure for all--it was impossible because the means of production would not suffice to create abundance for all even if all without exception laboured with all their physical power; and therefore much less would they have sufficed if the workers had indulged in the leisure which is as necessary to the development of the higher intellectual powers as abundance is to the maturing of the higher intellectual needs. And since it was not possible to guarantee to all the means of living a life worthy of human beings, it remained a sad, but not less inexorable, necessity of civilisation that the majority of men should be stinted even in the little that fell to their share, and that the booty snatched from the masses should be used to endow a minority who might thus attain to abundance and leisure. Servitude was a necessity of civilisation, because that alone made possible the development of the tastes and capacities of civilisation in at least a few individuals, while without it barbarism would have been the lot of all.

It is, moreover, a mistake to suppose that servitude is as old as the human race: it is only as old as civilisation. There was a time when servitude was unknown, when there were neither masters nor servants, and no one could exploit the labour of his fellow-men; that was not the Golden, but the Barbaric, Age of our race. While man had not yet learnt the art of *producing* what he needed, but was obliged to be satisfied with gathering or capturing the voluntary gifts of nature, and every competitor was therefore regarded as an enemy who strove to get the same goods which each individual looked upon as his own special prey, so long did the struggle for existence among men necessarily issue in reciprocal destruction instead of subjection and exploitation. It did not then profit the stronger or the more cunning to force the weaker into his service--the competitor had to be killed; and as the struggle was accompanied by hatred and superstition, it soon began to be the practice to eat the slain. A war of extermination waged by all against all, followed generally by cannibalism, was therefore the primitive condition of our race.

This first social order yielded, not to moral or philosophical considerations, but to a change in the character of labour. The man who first thought of sowing corn and reaping it was the deliverer of mankind from the lowest, most sanguinary stage of barbarism, for he was the first producer--he first practised the art not only of collecting, but of producing, food. When this art so improved as to make it possible to withdraw from the worker a part of his produce without positively exposing him to starvation, it was gradually found to be more profitable to use the vanquished as beasts of labour than as beasts for slaughter. Since slavery thus for the first time made it possible for at least a favoured few to enjoy abundance and leisure, it became the first promoter of higher civilisation. But civilisation is power, and so it came about that slavery or servitude in one form or another spread over the world.

But it by no means follows that the domination of servitude must, or even can, be perpetual. Just as cannibalism--which was the result of that minimum productiveness of human labour by means of which the severest toil sufficed to satisfy only the lowest animal needs of life--had to succumb to servitude as soon as the increasing productiveness of labour made any degree of abundance possible, so servitude--which is nothing else but the social result of that medium measure of productiveness by which labour is able to furnish abundance and leisure to a few but not to all--*must* also succumb to another, a higher social order, as soon as this medium measure of productiveness is surpassed, for from that moment servitude has ceased to be a necessity of civilisation, and has become a hindrance to its progress.

And for generations this has actually been the case. Since man has succeeded in making the forces of nature serviceable in production--since he has acquired the power of substituting the unlimited elemental forces for his own muscular force--there has been nothing to prevent his creating abundance and leisure for all; nothing except that obsolete social institution, servitude, which withholds from the masses the enjoyment of abundance and leisure. We not merely can, but we shall be compelled to make social justice an actual fact, because the new form of labour demands this as imperatively as the old forms of labour demanded servitude. Servitude, once the vehicle of progress, has become a hindrance to civilisation, for it prevents the full use of the means of civilisation at our disposal. As it reduces to a minimum the things consumed by most of our brethren, and therefore does not call into play more than a very small part of our present means of production, it compels us to restrict our productive labour within limits far less than those to which we should attain if an effective demand existed for what would then be the inevitable abundance of all kinds of wealth.

I sum up thus: Economic equality of rights could not be realised in earlier epochs of civilisation, because human labour was not then sufficiently productive to supply wealth to all, and equality therefore meant poverty for all, which would have been synonymous with barbarism. Economic equality of rights not only can but *must* now become a fact, because--thanks to the power which has been acquired of using the forces of nature--abundance and leisure have become possible for all; but the full utilisation of the now acquired means of civilisation is dependent on the condition that everyone enjoys the product of his own industry.

Satza-Muni (*Right*): I think it has been incontrovertibly shown that economic equality of rights was formerly impossible, and that it *can* now be realised; but why it *must* now be realised does not seem to me to have been yet placed beyond a doubt. So long as the productiveness of labour was small, the exploitation of man by man was a necessity of civilisation--that is plain; this is no longer the case, since the increased productiveness of labour is now capable of creating wealth enough for all--this is also as clear as day. But this only proves that economic justice has become possible, and there is a great difference between the possible and the necessary existence of a state of things. It has been said--and the experience of the exploiting world seems to justify the assertion--that full use cannot be made of the control which science and invention have given to men over the natural forces, while only a small part of the fruits of the thus increased effectiveness of labour is consumed; and if this can be irrefutably shown to be inherent in the nature of the thing, there remains not the least doubt that servitude in any form has become a hindrance to civilisation. For an institution that prevents us from making use of the means of civilisation which we possess is in and of itself a hindrance to civilisation; and since it restrains us from developing wealth to the fullest extent possible, and wealth and civilisation are power, so there can consequently be no doubt as to why and in what manner such an institution must in the course of economic evolution become obsolete. The advanced and the strong everywhere and necessarily imposes its laws and institutions upon the unprogressive and the weak; economic justice would therefore--though with bloodless means--as certainly and as universally supplant servitude as formerly servitude--when it was the institution which conferred a higher degree of civilisation and power--supplanted cannibalism. I have already admitted that the modern exploiting society is in reality unable to produce that wealth which would correspond to the now existing capacity of production: hence it follows as a matter of fact that the exploiting society is very much less advanced than one based upon the principle of economic justice, and it also quite as incontrovertibly follows that the former cannot successfully compete with the latter.

But before we have a right to jump to the conclusion that the principles of economic justice must necessarily be everywhere victorious, it must be shown that it is the essential nature of the exploiting system, and not certain transitory accidents connected with it, which makes it incapable of calling forth all the capacity of highly productive labour. Why is the existing exploiting society not able to call forth all this capacity? Because the masses are prevented from increasing their consumption in a degree corresponding to the increased power of production--because what is produced belongs not to the workers but to a few employers. Right. But, it would be answered, these few would make use of the produce themselves. To this the rejoinder is that that is impossible, because the few owners of the produce of labour can use--that is, actually consume--only the smallest portion of such an enormous amount of produce; the surplus, therefore, must be converted into productive capital, the employment of which, however, is dependent upon the consumption of those things that are produced by it. Very true. No factories can be built if no one wants the things that would be manufactured in them. But have the masters really only this *one* way of disposing of the surplus--can they really make no other use of it? In the modern world they do as a matter of fact make no other use of it. As a rule, their desire is to increase or improve the agencies engaged in labour--that is, to capitalise their profits--without inquiring whether such an increase or improvement is needed; and since no such increase is needed, so over-production--that is, the non-disposal of the produce--is the necessary consequence. But because this is the fact at present, *must* it necessarily be so? What if the employers of labour were to perceive the true relation of things, and to find a way of creating an equilibrium by proportionally reducing their capitalisation and increasing their consumption? If that were to happen, then, it must be admitted, all products would be disposed of, however much the productiveness of labour might increase. The consumption by the masses would be stationary as before; but luxury would absorb all the surplus with exception of such reserves as were required to supply the means of production, which means would themselves be extraordinarily increased on account of the enormously increased demand caused by luxury.

And who will undertake to say that such a turn of affairs is altogether impossible? The luxury of the few, it is said, cannot possibly absorb the immense surplus of modern productiveness. But why not? Because a rich man has only one stomach and one body; and, moreover, everyone cannot possibly have a taste for luxury. Granted; luxury, in its modern forms, cannot possibly consume more than a certain portion of the surplus produce of modern labour. But are we shut up to these modern kinds of luxury? What if the wealthy once more have recourse to a mode of spending repeatedly indulged in by antiquity in order to dispose of the accumulating proceeds of slave-labour? In ancient Egypt a single king kept 200,000 men busy for thirty years building his sepulchre, the great pyramid of Ghizeh. This same Pharaoh probably built also splendid palaces and temples with a no less profligate expenditure of human labour, and amassed treasures in which infinite labour was crystallised. Contemporaneously with him, there were other Egyptian magnates, priests, and warriors in no small number, who sought and found in similar ways employment for the labour of their slaves. If the luxury of the living did not consume enough, then costly spices, drink-offerings and burnt-offerings were lavished upon the dead, and thus the difficulty of disposing of the accumulated produce of labour was still further lightened. And this succeeded admirably. The Egyptian slave received a few onions and a handful of parched corn for food, a loin-cloth for clothing; and yet, notwithstanding a comparatively highly developed productiveness of the labour of countless slaves exploited by a few masters, there was no over-production. In ancient India the men in power excavated whole ranges of hills into temples, covered with the most exquisite sculptures, in which an infinite amount of labour was consumed; in ancient Rome the lords of the world ate nightingales' tongues, or instituted senseless spectacles, in order to find employment for the superfluous labour of countless slaves who, despite the considerable productiveness of labour, were kept in a condition of the deepest misery. And it answered. Why should not such a course answer in modern times? Because, thanks to the control we have acquired over nature, the productiveness of labour has become infinitely greater. Labour may have become infinitely more productive; indeed, I think it probable that it is no longer possible for the maddest prodigality of the few wealthy to give *full* employment to the whole of the labour-energy at present existing without admitting the masses to share in the consumption; but it would be possible for the wealthy to consume a very large portion of the possible produce. Then why does the modern exploiting society build no pyramids, no rock palaces; why do the lords of labour institute no costly cultus of the dead; why do they not eat nightingales' tongues, and keep the exploited populace busy with circus spectacles and mock sea-fights? They could indulge in these and countless other things, if they only discovered that the surplus must be consumed and not capitalised. But as long as they continue to multiply the instruments of labour, and only the instruments of labour, so long are they simply increasing over-production, and can become richer only in proportion as the consumption accidentally increases. As soon, however, as they adopt the above-mentioned expedient, the connection between their wealth and the lot of the masses is broken. Why does not this happen?

I hope it is not necessary for me expressly to assert that I am far from wishing for such a turn in affairs; rather, I should look upon it as the greatest misfortune that could befall mankind, for it would mean that, despite the enormously increased productiveness of labour, exploitation was not necessarily a hindrance to civilisation, and consequently would not necessarily be superseded by economic justice. But Confucius says rightly, that what is to be deplored is not always to be regarded as impossible or even as only improbable.

John Bell (*Centre*): The last speaker, who in other respects shows himself to be a profound thinker, overlooks the fact that the completest utilisation of the existing means of civilisation and the corresponding evolution of wealth are not the only determining criteria in the struggle for existence among nations. The strength of a nation that employs its wealth in fostering the higher development of the millions of its subjects, will ultimately become very different from that of a nation which consumes an equal amount of wealth merely in increasing the enjoyment, nay, the senseless luxury, of the ruling classes.

Aristid-Kolotroni (*Centre*): The last speaker is correct in what he says, although it may be objected that the wealthy are not necessarily obliged to consume their wealth in senseless luxury: they might just as well gratify their pride by boundless benevolence, accompanied by enormous expenditure in all imaginable kinds of scientific, artistic and other institutions of national utility. But I think we are getting away from the main point, which is: is such a turn of affairs possible? The fact that it has not occurred, despite all the evils of over-production, that on the contrary a continually growing desire to capitalise all surplus profits dominates the modern world, should save us from a fear of such a contingency.

Kurt Olafsohn (*Freeland*): I must agree with Satza-Muni, the honourable member for Japan, so far as to admit that the bare fact that such a contingency has not yet been realised cannot set our minds completely at rest. The consideration advanced by the two following speakers as to whether an exploiting society in which the consumption by the wealthy increases indefinitely must, under all circumstances, succumb to the influence of the free order of society, appears arbitrary and inconclusive. I venture to think that the free society does not possess the aggressive character of the exploiting society, and that therefore the latter, even though it should prove to be decidedly the weaker of the two, may continue to exist for some time side by side with the other so far as it does not itself recognise the necessity of passing over to the other. And this recognition would be materially delayed by the fact that the ruling classes profit by the continuance of exploitation. The change could then be effected universally only by sanguinary conflicts, whilst we lay great stress upon the winning over of the wealthy to the side of the reformers. It is the enormous burden of over-production that opens the eyes of exploiters to the folly of their action; should this spur be lacking, the beneficial revolution would be materially delayed. The member for Japan is also correct in saying that repeatedly in the course of history the surplus production which could not be consumed in a reasonable manner has led the exploiting lords of labour to indulge in senseless methods of consumption. It may therefore be asked whether what has repeatedly happened cannot repeat itself once more; but a thorough investigation of the subject will show that the question must be answered with a decided *No*.

No, it *can* never happen again that full employment for highly productive labour will be found except under a system of economic justice; for since it last occurred, a new factor has entered into the world which makes it for all times an impossibility. This factor is the mobilisation of capital and the consequent separation of the process of capital formation from the process of capital-using. Anyone who in Ancient Egypt or Ancient Rome had surplus production to dispose of and wished to invest it profitably, therefore in the form of aids to labour, must either himself have had a need of aids to labour, or must have found someone else who had such a need and was on that account prepared to take his surplus, at interest of course. It was impossible for anyone to invest capital unless someone could make use of such capital; and if this latter contingency did not occur, it was a matter of course that the possessor of the surplus production, unusable as capital, should seek some other mode of consuming it. Many such modes offered themselves, differing according to the nature of the several kinds of exploiting society. If the constitution of the commonwealth was a patriarchal one, the labour which had become more productive would be utilised in improving the condition of the serfs, in mitigating the severity of their labour. In a commonwealth of a more military character the increasing productiveness of labour would serve to enlarge the non-labouring, weapon-bearing class. If--as was always the case when civilisation advanced--the bond between lord and serf became laxer, the lord merely increased his luxury. But, in any case, the surplus which could not be utilised in the augmentation or improvement of labour was consumed, and there could therefore be no over-production. As now, however, the possessor of surplus produce can--even when no one has a need of his savings--obtain what he wants, viz. interest, he has ceased to concern himself as to whether that surplus is really required for purposes of production, but is anxious to capitalise even that which others can make as little use of as he can.

And this, in reality, is the result of the mobilisation of capital. Since this discovery has been made, all capital is as it were thrown into one lump, the profits of capital added to it, and the whole divided among the capitalists. No one needs my savings, they are absolutely superfluous, and can bear no fruit of any kind; nevertheless I receive my interest, for the mobilisation of capital enables me to share in the profits of profit-bearing, that is, of really working, capital. I deposit my savings at interest in a bank, or I buy a share or a bill and thereby raise the price of all other shares or bills correspondingly, and thus make it appear as if the capital which they represent had been increased, while in truth it has remained unchanged. And the produce of this working capital has not increased through the apparent addition of my capital; the interest paid on the whole amount of capital including mine is not more than that paid on the capital before mine was added to it. The addition of my superfluous capital has lowered the *rate* of interest, or, what comes to the same thing, has raised the price of a demand for the same rate of interest as before; but even a diminished rate of interest is better than no interest at all. I continue, therefore, to save and capitalise, despite the fact that my savings cannot be used productively as capital; nay, the above-mentioned diminution of the rate of interest impels me, under certain circumstances, to save yet more carefully, that is, to diminish my consumption in proportion as my savings become less remunerative. It is evident that my surplus produce cannot find any productive employment at all, yet there is no way out of this circle of over production. Luxury cannot come in as a relief, because the absence of any profitable employment for the surplus renders that surplus valueless, and the ultimate result is the non-production of the surplus. Only exceptionally is there an actual production of unconsumable and, consequently, valueless things; the almost unbroken rule is that the things which no one can use, and which therefore are valueless, will not be produced. Since the employer leaves to the worker only a bare subsistence, and can apply to capitalising purposes only so much as is required for the production of consumable commodities, every other application of the profits being excluded by capitalism, he cannot produce more than is enough to meet these two demands. If he attempts to produce more, the inevitable result is not increased wealth, but a crisis.

We have, therefore, no ground to fear that the ruling classes will again, as in pro-capitalistic epochs, be able to enjoy the fruits of the increasing productiveness of labour without allowing the working masses to participate in that enjoyment. Capitalism, though by no means--as some socialistic writers have represented--the cause of exploitation, is the obstacle which deprives modern society of every other escape from the fatal grasp of over-production but that of a transition to economic justice. It is the last stage in human economics previous to that of social justice. From capitalism there is no way forward but towards social justice; for capitalism is at one and the same time one of the most effectual provocatives of productivity and the bond which indissolubly connects the increase of the effective production of wealth with consumption.

Wilhelm Ohlms (*Right*): Then how is it that the Freeland institutions, which are to become those of the whole of civilised mankind, have broken with capitalism?

Henri Farr (*Freeland*): So far as by capitalism is to be understood the conversion of any actual surplus production into working capital, we in Freeland are far from having broken with it. On the contrary, we have developed it to the utmost, for much more fully than in the exploiting capitalistic society are our savings at all times at the disposal of any demand for capital that may arise. But our method of accumulating and mobilising capital is a very different and much more perfect one: the solidarity of interest of the saver with that of the employer of capital takes the place of interest. This form of capitalism can never lead to over-production, for under it--as in the pre-capitalistic epoch--it is the demand for capital that gives the first impulse to the creation of capital. But that this kind of capitalisation is impracticable in an exploiting society needs no proof. For such a society there is no other means of making the spontaneously accumulating capital serviceable to production than that of interest; and as soon as the mobilisation of capital dissolves the immediate personal connection between saver and employer of capital, creditor and debtor, interest inevitably impels to over-production, from which there is no escape except in economic justice--or relapse into barbarism. [Loud and general applause.]

The President here asked if anyone else wished to speak upon point 1 of the Agenda; and, as no one rose, he declared the discussion upon this subject closed.

The Congress next proceeded to discuss point 2:--

Is not the success of the Freeland institutions to be attributed merely to the accidental and therefore probably transient co-operation of specially favourable circumstances; or do those institutions rest upon conditions universally present and inherent in human nature?

George Dare (*Right*) opened the debate: We have the splendid success of a first attempt to establish economic justice so tangibly before us in Freeland, that there is no need to ask whether such an attempt *can* succeed. It is another question whether it *must* succeed, and that everywhere, because it has succeeded in this one case. For the circumstances of Freeland are exceptional in more than one respect. Not to mention the pre-eminent abilities, the enthusiasm and the spirit of self-sacrifice which marked the men who founded this fortunate commonwealth, and some of whom still stand at its head, men such as it is certain will not everywhere be found ready at hand, it must not be overlooked that this country is more lavishly endowed by nature than most others, and that a broad band of desert and wilderness protected it--at least at first--from any disturbing foreign influence. If men of talent, enjoying the unqualified confidence of their colleagues, are able on a soil where every seed bears fruit a hundredfold to effect the miracle of conjuring inexhaustible wealth for millions out of nothing, of exterminating misery and vice, of developing the arts and sciences to the fullest extent,--all this is, in my opinion, no proof that ordinary men, given perhaps to squabbling with each other, and to being mutually distrustful, will achieve the like or even approximately similar results on poorer land and in the midst of the turmoil of the world's competitive struggle. My doubts upon this point will appear the more reasonable when it is remembered that in America we have witnessed hundreds upon hundreds of social experiments which have all either proved to be in a greater or less degree miserable fiascos, or at least have only assumed the proportion of isolated successful industrial enterprises. It is true that some of our efforts at revolutionising modern society have had remarkable pecuniary results; but that has been all: a new, practicable foundation of the social organisation they have not furnished, not even in germ. I wished to give expression to these doubts; and before allowing ourselves to be intoxicated by the example of Freeland, I wished to invite you to a sober consideration of the question whether that which is successful in Freeland must necessarily succeed in the rest of the world.

Thomas Johnston (*Freeland*): The previous speaker makes a mistake when he ascribes the success of the Freeland undertaking to exceptionally favourable conditions. That our soil is more fertile than that of most other parts of the world is, it is true, a permanent advantage, which, however, accrues to us merely in the item of cost of carriage; for, after allowing for this, the advantage of the fertility of our soil is equally shared by all of you everywhere, wherever railways and steam-vessels can be made use of. Isolation from the market of the world by broad deserts was at first an advantage; but it would now be a disadvantage if we had not made ourselves masters of those deserts. And as to the abilities of the Freeland government, I must--not out of modesty, but in the name of truth--decline the compliments paid us. We are not abler than others whom you might find by the dozen in any civilised country. Only in one point were we in advance of others, namely, in perceiving what was the true basis of human economics. But the advantage which this gave us was only a temporary one, for at present you have men in abundance in every part of the civilised world who have become as wise as we are even in this matter. The advantage we derived from being the first in this movement was that we have enjoyed for nearly a generation the happiness in which you are only now preparing to participate. Freeland's advantages are due simply to the date of its foundation, and have now lost their importance. Now that the establishment of a world-wide freedom is contemplated, there will no longer be any national advantages or disadvantages. What belongs to us belongs to you also, and what is wonderful is that we as well as you will become richer in proportion as each of us is obliged to allow all the others to share quickly, easily, and fully our own wealth. We have suffered from being compelled to enjoy our wealth alone, and we shall become richer as soon as you share that wealth; and in the same way will you become richer as others share in your wealth. For herein lies the solidarity of interest that is associated with true freedom, that every existing advantage in production-- such as wealth is--can be the more fully utilised the wider the circle of those who enjoy its fruits.

That those attempts, of which the last speaker spoke, all miscarried is due to the fact that they were all based upon wrong principles. The only thing they have in common with what we have carried out in Freeland, and what you now wish to imitate, is the endeavour to find a remedy for the misery of the exploiting world; but the remedy which we seek is a different one from that which they sought, and in that--not in exceptional advantages which we may have had--lies the cause of our success and of their miscarriage.

For it was not by the aid of economic justice that they sought to attain their end; they sought deliverance from the dungeon of exploitation, whether by a way which did not lead out of it, or by a way which, though it led out of that dungeon, yet led into another and more dreadful one. In none of those American or other social experiments, from the Quaker colonies to the Icaria of Cabet, was the full and undiminished produce of labour ever assured to the worker; on the contrary, the produce belonged either to small capitalists who, while themselves taking part in the undertaking as workers, shared the produce according to the amount of capital they had invested, or it belonged to the whole as a body, who as such had a despotic right of disposal over both the labour and the produce of the labour of every individual. These reformers were, without exception, associated small capitalists or communists. They were able, if they had specially good fortune, or if they were under specially able direction, to achieve transient success; but a revolution of the current industrial system by them was not to be thought of.

(End of Second Day's Debate)

CHAPTER XXV

Third Day

(*Debate on Point 2 of the Agenda, continued*)

Johann Storm (*Right*): I think that the lack of any analogy between the frequent attempts to save society undertaken by small capitalists or communists and the institutions of Freeland has been made sufficiently clear. I think also that we are convinced that the exceptional external advantages, which may have at any rate favoured and assisted the success of Freeland, are not of a kind to suggest a fear that our proposed work will fail for the want of such advantages. But we do not yet know whether the success of social reform is exposed to danger from any conditions inherent in human nature, and therefore universally to be met with. We have, in our discussion upon the first point of the agenda, established the fact that, thanks to the control which has been acquired over the forces of nature, exploitation has become an obstacle to civilisation, and its removal a necessity of civilisation. But severe criticism cannot be satisfied with this. For is everything which is necessary to the progress of civilisation consequently also possible? What if economic justice, though an extraordinary vehicle of civilisation, were for some reason unfortunately impracticable? What if that marvellous prosperity, which astonishes us so much in Freeland, were only a transient phenomenon, and carried in itself the germ of decay, despite, nay, because of, its fabulous magnitude? In a word, what if mankind could not permanently, and as a whole, participate in that progress the necessary condition of which is economic justice?

The evidence to the contrary, already advanced, culminates in the proposition that the exploitation of man by man was necessary only so long as the produce of human labour did not suffice to provide abundance and leisure for all. But what if other influences made exploitation and servitude necessary, influences the operation of which could not be stayed by the increased productiveness of labour, perhaps could never be stayed? The most powerful hindrance to the permanent establishment of a condition of economic justice, with its consequences of happiness and wealth, is recognised by the anxious student of the future in the danger of over-population. But as this is a special point in the agenda, I, like my colleagues who have already spoken, will postpone what occurs to my mind upon the subject. There are, however, other and not less important difficulties. Can a society, which lacks the stimulus of self-interest, permanently exist and make progress, and succeed in making public spirit and rational enlightenment take the place thoroughly, and with equal effectiveness, of self-interest? Does not the same apply to private property? Self-interest and private property are not altogether set aside by the institutions of Freeland. I readily admit this, but they are materially restricted. Even under the rule of economic justice the individual is himself responsible for the greater or less degree of his prosperity--the connection between what he himself does and what he gets is not altogether dissolved; but as the commonwealth unconditionally protects every man in all cases against want, therefore against the ultimate consequences of his own mistakes or omissions, the stimulating influence of self-responsibility is very materially diminished. Just so we see private property abolished, though not entirely, yet in its most important elements. The earth and all the natural forces inherent in it are declared ownerless; the means of production are common property; will that, can that, remain so everywhere, and for all time, without disastrous consequences? Will public spirit permanently fill the office of that affectionate far-seeking care which the owner bestows upon the property for which he alone is responsible? Will not the gladsome absence of care, which has certainly hitherto been brilliantly conspicuous in Freeland, eventually degenerate into frivolity and neglect of that for which no one in particular is responsible? The fact that this has not yet happened may perhaps be due--for it is not yet a generation since this commonwealth was founded--to the dominant enthusiasm that marked the beginning. New brooms, it is said, sweep clean. The Freelander sees the eyes of the whole world fixed upon him and his doings; he feels that he is still the pioneer of new institutions; he is proud of those institutions, every worker here to the last man holds himself responsible for the way and manner in which he fulfils the apostolate of universal freedom to which he is called. Will this continue permanently: in particular, will the whole human race feel and act thus? I doubt it; at least, I am not fully convinced that it must necessarily be so. And what if it is not so? What if, we will not say all, but many nations show themselves to be unable to dispense with the stimulus of want-inspired self-interest, the lure of unconditioned private property, without sinking into mental stagnation and physical indolence? These are questions to which we now require answers.

Richard Held (*Centre*): The previous speaker finds that self-interest and private property are such powerful spurs to activity that, without their full and unrestricted influence, permanent human progress is scarcely conceivable, and that it is extremely uncertain whether public spirit would be an effective substitute for them. I go much farther. I assert that without these two means of activity no commonwealth can be expected to thrive, unless human nature is radically changed, or labour ceases to require effort.

Every attempt in the domain of economics to substitute public spirit or any other ethical motive for self-interest must immediately, and not merely in its ultimate issue, prove an ignominious fiasco. I think it quite unnecessary to give special proof of this; but for the very reason that self-interest and its correlative, private property, are the best incitements to labour, and can be effectively replaced by no surrogate--for this very reason, I contend, are the institutions of economic justice immensely superior in this respect to those of the exploiting system of industry. For they alone really give full play to self-interest and the right of private ownership: the exploiting system only falsely pretends to do this.

For servitude is, in truth, the negation of self-interest. Self-interest assumes that the worker serves his 'own' interest by the trouble he takes; does this apply to the *régime* of exploitation: does the servant work for his *own* profit? With reference to the question of self-interest, anyone who would show that economic justice was less advantageous than servitude would have to assert that labour was the most productive and profitable when the worker produced, not for his own, but for some one else's profit. But it will perhaps be objected that the employer produces for his own profit. Right. But, apart from the fact that this, strictly speaking, has nothing to do with the stimulating effect of self-interest upon labour--for here it is not the profit of his own but of some one else's labour that comes in question--it is clear that a system which secures to only a minority the profit of work must be infinitely less influential than the one we are now considering, which secures the profit to every worker. In reality the exploiting world, with very few exceptions, knows only men who labour without getting the profit themselves, and men who do not labour themselves yet get profit from labour; in the exploiting world to labour for one's own profit is quite an accidental occurrence. With what right, then, does exploitation dare to plume itself upon making use of *self*-interest as a motive to labour? *Some one else's* interest is the right description of the motive to labour that comes into play under exploitation; and that this should prove itself to be more effective than the self-interest which economic justice has to introduce into the modern world as a novelty it would be somewhat difficult to demonstrate.

It is nearly the same with private property. What boundless presumption it is to claim for a system which robs ninety-nine per cent. of mankind of all and every certainty of possessing property, and leaves to them nothing that they can call their own but the air they breathe--what presumption it is to claim for such a system that it makes use of private property as a stimulus to human activity, and to urge this claim as against another system which converts all men without exception into owners of property, and in fact secures to them unconditionally, and without diminution, all that they are able in any way to produce! Or does, perhaps, the superiority of the 'private property' of the exploiting system lie in the fact that it extends to things which the owner has *not* himself produced? Unquestionably the adherents of the old system have no clear conception of what is *mine* and what is *thine*. What properly belongs to *me*? 'Everything you can take from anyone, 'would be their only answer, if they were but to speak honestly. Because this appropriation of the property of others has, in the course of thousands of years, been formulated into certain established rules, consecrated by cruel necessity, the adherents of the old system have completely lost the natural conception of private property, the conception which is inherent in the nature of things. It passes their comprehension that, though force can possess and make use of whom it pleases, yet the free and untrammelled use of one's own powers is the inalienable property of everyone, and that consequently any political or social system which overrides this inalienable personal right of every man is based, not upon property, but upon robbery. This robbery may be necessary, nay, useful--we have seen that for thousands of years it actually was useful--but 'property' it never will be, and whoever thinks it is has forgotten what property is.

After what has been said, it seems to me scarcely necessary to spend many words in dispelling the fear that frivolity or carelessness in the treatment of the means of production will result from a modified form of property. As to frivolity, it will suffice to ask whether hopeless misery has proved itself to be such a superior stimulus to economic prudence as to make it dangerous to supersede it by a personal responsibility which, though it lacks the spur of misery, is of a thoroughly comprehensive character. And as to the fear lest carelessness in the treatment of the means of production should prevail, this fear could have been justified only if in the former system the workers were owners of the means of production. Private property in these will, it is true, not be given to them by the new system, but instead of it the undiminished enjoyment of the produce of those means; and he whose admiration of the beauties of the existing system does not go so far as to consider the master's rod a more effective stimulus to foresight than the profit of the workers may rest satisfied that even in this respect things will be better and not worse.

Charles Phud (*Right*): I do not at all understand how the previous speaker can dispute the fact that in the former system self-interest is that which conditions the quantity of work. No one denies that the workers must give up a part of the profit of their labour; but another part remains theirs, hence they labour for their own profit, though not exclusively so. At any rate they must labour if they do not wish to starve, and one would think that this stimulus is the most effectual one possible. So much as to the denial that self-interest is the moving spring of so-called exploited labour. As to the attack upon the conception of property advanced by those of us who defend, not exactly the existing evil condition of things, but a rational and consistent reform of it, I would with all modesty venture to remark that our sense of justice was satisfied because no one compelled the worker to share with the employer. He made a contract as a free man with the employer.... [General laughter.] You may laugh, but it is so. In countries that are politically free nothing prevents the worker from labouring on his own account alone; it is, therefore, at any rate incorrect to call the portion which he surrenders to the employer robbery.

Béla Székely (*Centre*): It seems to me to be merely a dispute about a word which the previous speaker has attempted to settle. He calls wages a part of the profit of production. It may be that here and there the workers really receive a part of the profit as wages, or as an addition to the wages. With us, and, if I am rightly informed, in the country of the speaker also, this was not generally customary. We rather paid the workers, who were quite unconcerned about the profits of their work, an amount sufficient to maintain them; profits--and losses when there were any--fell exclusively to the lot of the production, the employers. He could have said with nearly as much justice that his oxen or his horses participated in the profits of production. When I say 'nearly,' I mean that this could as a rule be said *more* justly of oxen and horses, for, while those useful creatures are for the most part better fed when their labour has enriched their master, this happens very rarely in the case of our two-logged rational beasts of labour.

Then the previous speaker made hunger absolutely identical with self-interest. The masses *must* labour or starve. Certainly. But the slave must labour or be whipped: thus this strange logic would make it appear that the slave is also stimulated to labour by self-interest. Or will the arguer fall back upon the assertion that self-interest refers merely to the acquisition of material goods? That would be false; self-interest does not after all either more or less prompt men to avoid the whip than to appease hunger. But I will not argue about such trifles: we will drop the rod and the whip as symbols of activity stimulated by self-interest. But how does it stand with those slave-holders who--probably in the interest of the 'freedom of labour'--do not whip their lazy slaves, but allow them to starve? Is it not evident that the previous speaker would, under their *régime*, set self-interest upon the throne as the inciter to work? That hunger is a very effectual means of *compulsion*, a more effectual one than the whip, no one will deny; hence it has everywhere superseded the latter, and very much to the advantage of the employer. But self-interest? The very word itself implies that the profit of the labour is the worker's own. So much as to hunger.

And now as to the security against the injustice of exploitation; for my own part I do not understand this at all. The workers were 'free,' nothing compelled them to produce for other men's advantage? Yes, certainly, nothing but the trifle--hunger. They could leave it alone, if they wished to starve! Just the 'freedom' which the slave has. If he does not mind being whipped, there is nothing to compel him to work for his master. The bonds in which the 'free' masses of the exploiting society languish are tighter and more painful than the chains of the slave. The word 'robbery' does not please the previous speaker? It is, indeed, a hard and hateful word; but the 'robber' is not the individual exploiter, but the exploiting society, and this was formerly, in the bitter need of the struggle for existence, compelled to practise this robbery. Is the slaughter in battle any the less homicide because it is done at the command, not of the individual, but of the State, which is frequently acting under compulsion? It will be said that this kind of killing is not forbidden by the penal law, nay, that it is enjoined by our duty to our country, and that only forbidden kinds of killing can be called 'homicide.' *Juridically* that is quite correct; and if it occurred to anyone to bring a charge of killing in battle before a court of justice he would certainly be laughed at. But he would make himself quite as ludicrous who, because killing in war is allowed, would deny that such killing was homicide if the point under consideration was, not whether the act was juridically penal, but how to define homicide as a mode of violently putting a man to death. So exploitation is no robbery in the eye of the penal law; but if every appropriation to one's self of the property of another can be called robbery--and this is all that the present case is concerned with--then is robbery and nothing else the basis of every exploiting society, of the modern 'free' society no less than of the ancient or mediaeval slave-holding or serf-keeping societies. [Long-continued applause, in which Messrs. Johann Storm and Charles Prud both joined.]

James Brown (*Right*): Our colleague from Hungary has so pithily described the true characteristics of self-interest and property in the exploiting society, that nothing more is to be said upon that subject. But even if it is correct that these two motive springs of labour can be placed in their right position only by economic justice, it still remains to be asked whether the only way of doing this--namely, the organisation of free, self-controlling, unexploited labour--will prove to be everywhere and without exception practicable. Little would be gained by the solemn proclamation of the principle that every worker is his own master, and the complete concession to all workers of a right of disposal of the means of production, if those workers were to prove incapable of making an adequate use of such rights. The final and decisive question, therefore, is whether the workers of the future will always and everywhere exhibit that discipline, that moderation, that wisdom, which are indispensable to the organisation of truly profitable and progressive production? The exploiting industry has a routine which has taken many thousands of years for its development.

The accumulated experience of untold generations teaches the employer under the old system how to proceed in order to control a crowd of servants compelled dumbly to obey. He, nevertheless, frequently fails, and only too often are his plans wrecked by the insubordination of those under him. The leaders of the workers' associations of the future have as good as no experience to guide them in the choice of modes of association; they will have as masters those whom they should command, and yet we are told that success is certain, nay, success must be certain if the associated free society is not to be convulsed to its very foundations. For whilst the exploiting society confines the responsibility for the fate of the separate undertakings to those undertakings themselves, the so-often-mentioned solidarity of interests in the free society most indissolubly connects the weal and the woe of the community with that of every separate undertaking. I shall be glad to be taught better; but until I am, I cannot help seeing in what has just been said grounds for fear which the experience of Freeland until now is by no means calculated to dissipate. The workers of Freeland have understood how to organise and discipline themselves: does it follow from this that the workers everywhere will be equally intelligent?

Miguel Spada (*Left*): I will confine myself to a brief answer to the question with which the previous speaker closed. It certainly does not follow that the attempt to organise and discipline labour without capitalist employers must necessarily succeed among *all* nations simply because it has succeeded among the Freelanders, and will unquestionably succeed among numerous other peoples. It is possible, nay, probable, that some nations may show themselves incapable of making use of this highest kind of spontaneous activity; so much the worse for them. But I hope that no one will conclude from this that those peoples who are not thus incapable--even if they should find themselves in the minority--ought to refrain from such activity. The more capable will then become the instructors of the less capable. Should the latter, however, show themselves to be, not merely temporarily incapable, but permanently intractable, then will they disappear from the face of the earth, just as intractable cannibals must disappear when they come into contact with civilised nations. The delegate who proposed the question may rest assured that the nation to which he belongs will not be numbered among the incapable ones.

Vladimur Tonof (*Freeland*): The honourable member from England (Brown) has formed an erroneous conception of the difficulties of the organisation and discipline now under consideration, as well as of the importance of any miscarriage of individual enterprises in a free community. As to the former matter, I wish to show that in the organisation of associated capital, which is well known to have been carried out for centuries, there is an instructive and by no means to be despised foreshadowing of associated labour, so far as relates to the modes of management and superintendence to be adopted in such cases. Of course there are profound distinctions which have to be taken into consideration; but it has been proved, and it is in the nature of things, that the differences are all in favour of associated labour. In this latter, for instance, there will not be found the chief sins of associations of capitalists--namely, lack of technical knowledge and indifference to the objects of the undertaking on the part of the shareholders; and therefore it is possible completely to dispense with those useless and crippling kinds of control-apparatus with which the statutes of the companies of capitalists are ballasted. As a rule, the single shareholder understands nothing of the business of his company, and quite as seldom dreams of interfering in the affairs of the company otherwise than by receiving his dividends. Notwithstanding, *he* is the master of the undertaking, and in the last resort it is his vote that decides the fate of it; what provisions are therefore necessary in order to protect this shareholder from the possible consequences of his own ignorance, credulity, and negligence! The associated workers, on the contrary, are fully acquainted with the nature of their undertaking, the success of which is their chief material interest, and is, without exception, recognised as such by them. This is a decisive advantage. Or does anyone see a special difficulty in the fact that the workers are placed under the direction of persons whose appointment depends upon the votes of the men who are to be directed? On the same ground might the authority of all elective political and other posts be questioned. The directors have no means of *compelling* obedience? A mistake; they lack only the right of arbitrarily dismissing the insubordinate. But this right is not possessed by many other bodies dependent upon the discipline and the reasonable co-operation of their members; nevertheless, or rather on this very account, such bodies preserve better discipline than those confederations in which obedience is maintained by the severest forcible measures. It is true that where there is no forcible compulsion discipline cannot so easily pass over into tyranny; but this is, in truth, no evil. Moreover, the directors of free associations of workers can put into force a means of compulsion, the power of which is more unqualified and absolute than that of the most unmitigated tyranny: the all-embracing reciprocal control of the associates, whose influence even the most obstinate cannot permanently withstand. It is certainly indispensable that the workers as a whole, or a large majority of them, should be reasonable men whose intelligence is sufficient to enable them to understand their own interests. But this is the first and foremost *conditio sine quâ non* of the establishment of economic justice. That economic justice--up to the present the highest outcome of the evolution of mankind--is suitable only to men who have raised themselves out of the lowest stage of brutality, is in no respect open to question. Hence it follows that nations and individuals who have not yet reached this stage of development must be educated up to it; and this educational work is not difficult if it be but undertaken with a will. We doubt that it could altogether fail anywhere, if undertaken seriously and in the right way.

And now let us look at the second side of the question which has been thrown out. Is it correct that, in consequence of the solidarity of interests which exists in the free community, the weal and woe of the whole are indissolubly bound up with the success of any individual undertaking? If it be meant by this that in such a community everyone is interested in the weal of everyone else, and consequently in the success of every undertaking, then it fully expresses what is the fact; but--and this was evidently the meaning of the speaker--if it is meant that the weal of such a community is dependent upon the success of every single undertaking of its members, then it is utterly groundless. If an undertaking does not thrive, its members leave it and turn to one that is more prosperous--that is all. On the other hand, this mobility of labour, bound up with the solidarity of interests, protects the free community from the worse consequences of actual miscarriage. If there should be an ill-advised choice of directors, the unqualified officials can do but relatively little mischief; they see themselves--that is, the undertaking under their control--promptly forsaken by the workers, and the losses are insignificant because confined within a small area. In fact, this mobility proves itself to be in the last resort the most effectual corrective of all kinds of mistakes, the agency by which all the defective forms of organisation and the less capable minds are thrust aside and automatically superseded by better. For the undertakings which, from any cause whatever, fail to thrive are always in a comparatively short time absorbed by better, without involving in ruin--as happens under the exploiting system of society--those who were engaged in the former undertakings. Hence it is not necessary that these free organisations should in all cases strike the highest note at the very beginning in order eventually to attain to perfect order and excellence; for in the friendly competition what is defective rapidly vanishes from sight, being merged in what is proved to be superior, which then alone holds the field.

John Kilmean (*Right*): Let us grant, then, that the associations of free labour are organised as well as, or better than, the capitalists' associations of the old exploiting world. Is there, nevertheless, no ground to fear that they will exhibit serious defects in comparison with undertakings conducted by individual employers? That self-interest, so far as concerns the workers themselves, can for the first time have full play in stimulating activity is true; but with respect to the management the reverse is the fact. At least one would think that the interest of the individual undertaker in the success of the business belonging to him alone must be a keener one than that of directors, who are nothing more than elected functionaries whose industrial existence is in no way indissolubly connected with the undertaking. The advantages which the private undertaking conducted by the individual proprietor has hitherto exhibited over the joint-stock company, it must, in the nature of things, also have over the free associations.

Theodor Ypsilanti (*Freeland*): Let us assume, for the present, that this is so. But are the advantages of the individual undertaker over the joint-stock company really so great? It is not necessary to theorise for and against, since practice has long ago pronounced its verdict. And what is this? Simply that the joint-stock undertaking has gradually surpassed, nay, in the most important and the most extensive branches of business totally superseded, the much-lauded private undertaking. It can be confidently assorted that in every kind of undertaking which is large enough to support the--certainly somewhat costly--apparatus of a joint-stock company, the joint-stock company is undisputed master of the field, so that there remains to the private undertaking, as its domain, nothing more than the dwarf concerns with which our free society does not meddle. It cannot be said that this is due to the larger money power of the combined capital, for even relatively small undertakings, whose total capital is many times less than that of a great many private millionaires, prefer, I may say choose exclusively, the joint-stock form. It is quite as great a mistake to ascribe this fact to the reluctance of private capitalists to run the risk involved in certain undertakings, and to their consequent preference for joint-stock undertakings; for, in the first place, it is generally the least risky branches of business in which the joint-stock form most exclusively prevails; and in the second place, we see only too often that individual capitalists place enormous sums in single companies, and even found undertakings in a joint-stock form with their own capital. But a decisive proof of the superiority of the joint-stock company is the universal fact that the great capitalists are everywhere entrusting the control of their property to joint-stock companies. If the account-books of the wealthy in every civilised exploiting country were to be examined, it would unquestionably be found that at least nine-tenths of the capitalists had employed the greatest part of their capital which was not invested in land in the purchase of shares. This, however, simply shows that the rich prefer not to manage their wealth themselves, but to allow it to be managed by joint stock companies.

The orthodox theory, spun out of the flimsiest fictions, is not able to do anything with this fact; it therefore ignores it, or seeks to explain it by a number of fresh fictions, such as the fable of divided risk, or some other similar subterfuge. The truth is that the self-interest of the employer has very little to do with the real direction of the businesses belonging to him--so far as concerns great undertakings--for not the employer, but specially appointed wage-earners, are, as a rule, the actual directors; the alleged advantage of the private undertaking, therefore, does not exist at all. On the other hand, the undertaking of the private capitalist is at a very heavy disadvantage in competition with that of the joint-stock company, inasmuch as the latter almost always attracts by far the greater amount of intelligence. The capitalist, even the largest, is on the average no cleverer than other men- -that is, generally speaking, he is *not* particularly clever. It may, perhaps, be objected that he would scarcely have attained to great wealth had he not possessed superior abilities; but apart from the fact that it has yet to be established whether in the modern exploiting society it is really special mental gifts, and not rather other things, that lead to the accumulation of great wealth, most large fortunes are no longer in the hands of the original acquirers, but in those of their heirs. Consequently, in private undertakings, if not the actual direction, yet certainly the highest authority, and particularly the final decision as to the choice of the actual directors, lies in the hands of men who, shall we say, half of them, possess less than the average, nine-tenths of the rest about the average, and only one-twentieth of them more than the average of human intelligence. Naturally nineteen-twentieths of the undertakings thought out and established by such men will be either indifferent or bad. It will be further objected that it is in the main the same men to whom a similar *rôle* falls in the creation and officering of joint-stock companies. Very true. But here it is usual for the few able men among the wealthy to take the *rôle* of leaders; the stupid or the moderately gifted are changed from autocratic despots into a herd of common docile cattle, who, led by the instinct of self-interest, blindly follow the abler men. And even when it is otherwise, when the incapable rich man stubbornly insists upon thrusting forward his empty pate, he finds himself compelled to give reasons for what he does, to engage in the game of question and answer with his fellow shareholders, and ordinarily he is thus preserved from the gross follies which he would be sure to commit if the whole responsibility rested upon himself. In a word, capitalists acting together as joint-stock companies as a rule exhibit more ability than capitalists acting independently. But even if it were not so, the selections which they make--as shareholders--in appointing the chief managers of their business are infinitely better than those made by private capitalists, because a whole category of intelligences, and that of the highest and best kind, stands at the disposal of the joint-stock company, but not of the private undertaker. Many persons who offer themselves as directors, members of council of administration, presidents, of joint-stock companies, would never condescend to enter into the service of an individual. The general effect of all this is, that joint-stock companies in the greater number of cases possess far abler, more intelligent managers than private undertakings--a circumstance which no one will overlook who is but even moderately well acquainted with the facts of the case.

The alleged superiority of the private undertaking, supposed to be due to the personal care and oversight of the owner, is therefore nothing more than one of the many fables in which the exploiting world believes in spite of the most obvious lack of truth. But even the trifling advantages which the private undertaking really has over the joint-stock company cannot be claimed as against freely associated labour. Colleague Tonof has already pointed out that ignorance and indifference, those most dangerous characteristics of most shareholders, are not to be feared in those who take part in labour associations. Here it can never happen that an unscrupulous minority will obtain control of the management and exploit the undertaking for the benefit of some private interest; here it is natural that the whole body of members, who are interested in the successful conduct of the business, should incessantly and attentively watch the behaviour of the officials they have elected; and in view of the perfect transparency of all the business transactions in the free community, secret practices and crooked ways--those inevitable expedients of dishonour--are not to be thought of. In a word, the form of labour organisation corresponding to the higher stage of civilisation proves itself to be infinitely superior in every respect to the form of organisation prevalent in the past--a fact which, strictly speaking, is a matter of course.

It does not follow that this form of organisation is the most suitable for every kind of labour; there are branches of production--I mention merely the artistic or the scientific--in which the individual must stand by himself; but we do not apply the principle of association to these branches. For no one would forcibly impose this principle, and the individual freedom that is nowhere interfered with is able of itself to take care that what is done is everywhere done in the way that has been found to be most consistent with nature, and best.

Miguel Diego (*Right*): We know now that the new system unites in itself all the natural requisites of success; it has been shown before that its introduction was demanded by the progress of civilisation. How comes it that, in spite of all, the new system enters the world, not as the product of the co-operation of elementary automatically occurring historical events, but rather as a kind of art-product, as an artificially produced outcome of the efforts of certain individuals? What if the International Free Society had not been formed, or if its appeal had been without response, its work crushed in the germ, or in some other way made to miscarry? It will be admitted that these are conceivable contingencies. What would have become of economic justice if any one of these possibilities had occurred? If social reform is in truth an inevitable necessity, it must ultimately be realised in spite of the opposition of the whole world; it must show itself to be indissolubly bound up with forces which will give it the victory over prejudice, ill-will, and adverse accident. Thus alone would proof be given that the work in which we are engaged is something more than the ephemeral fruit of fallible human ingenuity--that rather those men who gave it the initial impulse and watched over its development were acting simply as the instruments of the universal force which, if *they* had not done the work, would have found other instruments and other ways to attain the inevitable end.

Henri Ney (*Freeland*): If the existence of economic justice as an established fact depended upon the action of the founders of Freeland, little could have been said, not merely as to its necessary character, but also as to the certainty of its continuance. For what individual men attempt, other men can frustrate. It is true that, as far as outward appearances go, all historical events are human work: but the great necessary events of history are distinguished from merely accidental occurrences by the fact that in them all the actors are clearly seen to be simply the instruments of destiny, instruments which the genius of mankind calls into being when it is in need of them. We do not know who invented language, the first tool, writing; but whoever it was, we know that he was a mere instrument of progress, in the sense that, with the same certainty with which we express any other natural law, we can venture to assert that language, the tool, writing, would have been invented even if their respective accidental inventors had never seen the light. The same holds good of economic freedom: it would have been realised, even if none of us who actually realised it for the first time had existed. Only in such a case the form of its entrance into the world of historical fact would probably have been a different, perhaps a more pacific, a more joyous one still than that of which we are the witnesses; but perhaps it might have been a violent and horrible one.

In order to show this in a manner that excludes all doubt, it must first be demonstrated that the continuance of modern society as it has been evolved in the course of the last century is in the very nature of things an impossibility. For this purpose you must allow me to carry you back some distance.

In the original society of barbarism, when the productiveness of labour was so small that the weaker could not be exploited by the stronger, and one's own prosperity depended upon the suppression and annihilation of competitors, a thirst for blood, cruelty, cunning, were not merely necessary to the self-preservation of the individual, but they were obviously serviceable to the society to which the individual belonged. They were, therefore, not only universally prevalent, but were reckoned as virtues. The most successful and most merciless slayer of men was the most honourable member of his tribe, and was lauded in speech and song as an example worthy of imitation.

When the productiveness of labour increased, these 'virtues' lost much of their original importance; but they were not converted into vices until slavery was invented, and it became possible to utilise the labour instead of the flesh of the conquered. Then bloodthirsty cruelty, which hitherto had been profitable, became injurious, since, for the sake of a transient enjoyment--that of eating human flesh--it deprived the victorious individual, as well as the society to which he belonged, of the permanent advantage of augmented prosperity and increased power. Consequently, the bestial thirst for blood gradually disappeared in the new form of the struggle for existence, and from a cherished virtue it passed into a characteristic which met with increasing disapproval--that is, it became a vice. It necessarily became a vice, for only those tribes which were the subjects of this process of moral transformation could enjoy all the advantages of the new forms of labour and of the new social institution, slavery, and could therefore increase in civilisation and power, and make use of their augmented power to extirpate or to bring into subjection the tribes that persisted in their old cannibal customs. In this way, in the course of thousands of years, there grew up among men a new ethics which, in its essential features, has been preserved until our days--the ethics of exploitation.

But to call this ethics 'philanthropy' is the strangest of mistakes. It is true that the savage bloodthirsty hatred between man and man had given place to milder sentiments; but it is a long way from those sentiments to genuine philanthropy, by which we understand the recognition of our fellow-man as our equal, and not merely that chilly benevolence which we entertain towards even dumb animals. Real philanthropy is as inconsistent with exploitation as with cannibalism. For though the new form of the struggle for existence abhors the death of the vanquished, it substitutes for it the oppression and subjugation of man by man as an imperative requirement of social prosperity. And it should be clearly understood that real and unselfish philanthropy is not merely not demanded by the kind of struggle for existence which is carried on by the exploiting society, but is known to be distinctly injurious, and is quite impracticable as a universally operative race-instinct. Individuals may love their fellow-men as themselves; but as long as exploitation is in force, such men must remain rare, and by no means generally esteemed, exceptions. Only hypocrisy or gross self-deception will question this. Certainly the so-called civilised nations of the West have for more than a thousand years written upon their banners the words 'Love thy neighbour as thyself,' and have not shrunk from asserting that they lived up to those words, or that at least they endeavoured to do so. But in truth they loved their fellow-man, in the best of cases, as a useful domestic animal, have without the slightest scruple profited by his painful toil, by his torture, and have not been prevented by any sentiment of horror from slaughtering him in cold blood when such a course was or seemed to be profitable to them. And such were not the sentiments and feelings of a few particularly hard-hearted individuals, but of the whole body of society; they were not condemned but imperatively demanded by public opinion, lauded as virtues under all sorts of high-sounding names, and, so far as deeds and not empty phrases were in question, their antithesis, the genuine philanthropy, passed at best as pitiable folly, or more generally as a crime worthy of death. He who uttered the words quoted above, and to Whom prayers were offered in the churches, would have been repeatedly crucified, burnt, broken on the wheel, hanged by them all, in the most recent past perhaps imprisoned, had He again ventured, as He did nineteen centuries ago, to preach in the market-place, in burning living words that could not be misunderstood, that which men's purblind eyes and their minds clouded by a thousand years of ancient self-deception read, but did not understand, in the writings of His disciples.

But the decisive point is, that in the epoch of exploitation mankind could not have thought or felt, not to say acted, otherwise. They were compelled to practise exploitation so long as this was a necessity of civilisation; they were therefore unable either to feel or exercise philanthropy, for that was as little in harmony with exploitation as repugnance to homicide was with cannibalism. Just as in the first barbaric epoch of mankind that which the exploiting period called 'humanity' would have been detrimental to success in the struggle for existence, so, later, that which *we* call humanity, the genuine philanthropy, would have placed any nation that had practised it at a disadvantage. To eat or to be eaten--that was the alternative in the epoch of cannibalism; to oppress or to be oppressed, in the epoch of exploitation.

A change in the form and productiveness of labour has recently been effected; neither social institutions nor moral sensibilities can escape the influence of that change. But--and here I come to the last decisive point--there are certainly several alternatives conceivable. The first is that with which we have hitherto been exclusively occupied: the social institutions accommodate themselves to the change in the form of labour, and the modification of the struggle for existence thus brought about leads to a corresponding revolution in moral sentiments; friendly competition and perfect solidarity of interests supersede the reciprocal struggle for advantage, and the highest philanthropy supersedes the exploitation of man.

If we would once for all remove the last doubt as to the unqualified necessity of this phase of evolution, let us suppose that the contrary has happened, that the adaptation of the social institutions to the modified form of labour is not effected. At any rate the mind can imagine such a possibility; and I hold it to be superfluous, at this point in the demonstration, to discuss the probability or the improbability of such a supposition--we simply assume the case. But it would be absurd likewise to assume that this persistence of the old form of the social institutions could occur without being necessarily accompanied by very material reactions both upon the forms of labour and upon the moral instincts of mankind. Those over-orthodox but not less thoughtless social politicians who accept the above assumption, hold it to be possible for a cause of such enormous and far-reaching importance as is an increased productiveness of labour, that makes it possible for all men to enjoy abundance and leisure, to remain without the slightest influence upon the course of human evolution. They overlook the fact that the struggle for existence in human society must in any case be changed under the influence of this factor, whether the social institutions undergo a corresponding adaptation or not, and that consequently the inquiry must in any case be made what reaction this changed form of the struggle for existence can or must exercise upon the totality of human institutions?

And in what consists the change in the struggle for existence, in such a case as that indicated above? *Simply in a partial reversion to the form of struggle of the first, the cannibal, epoch of mankind!*

We have seen that exploitation transformed the earlier struggle, that aimed at annihilating the competitor, into one directed towards his subjugation. But now, when the productiveness of labour is so great that the consumption, kept down by exploitation, is no longer able to follow it, the suppression, the--if not the physical, yet the industrial--annihilation of the competitor is once more a necessary condition of everyone's prosperity, and the struggle for existence assumes at once the forms of subjugation and annihilation. In the domain of industry it now profits little to have arbitrary authority over any number of human subjects of exploitation; if the exploiter is not able to drive his co-exploiter from the market, he must succumb in the struggle for existence. And the exploited now have not merely to defend themselves from the harsh treatment of their masters: they must, if they would ward off hunger, fight with tooth and claw for the only too few places at the food-crib in the 'labour market.' Is it conceivable that such a terrible alteration in the fundamental conditions of the struggle for existence can remain without influence upon human ethics? Cause and effect *must* correspond--the ethics of the cannibal epoch *must* triumphantly return. In consequence of the altered character of the conflict of annihilation, the former cruel and malicious instincts will undergo a modification, but the fundamental sentiment, the unqualified animosity against one's fellow-man, must return. During the thousands of years when the struggle was directed towards the making use of one's neighbour, and especially when the exploited had become accustomed to reverence in the exploiter a higher being, there was possible between master and servant at least that degree of attachment which exists between a man and his beast. Neither masters nor servants had any necessary occasion to hate each other. Mutual consideration, magnanimity, kindness, gratitude, could in such a condition become--certainly very sparingly--substitutes for philanthropy. But now, when exploitation and suppression are at one and the same time the watchwords of the struggle, the above-mentioned virtues must more and more assume the character of obstacles to a successful struggle for existence, and must consequently disappear in order to make room for mercilessness, cunning, cruelty, malice. And all these disgraceful characteristics must not merely become universally prevalent: they must also become universally esteemed, and be raised from the category of the most shameful kinds of baseness to that of 'virtues.' As little as it is possible to conceive of a 'humane' cannibal or of an exploiter under the influence of real philanthropy, so little is it possible to think of a magnanimous and--in the former sense--virtuous exploiter permanently under the colossal burden of over-production; and as certainly as the cannibal society was compelled to recognise the thirst for murder as the most praiseworthy of all virtues, so certainly must the exploiting society, cursed by over-production, learn to reverence the most cunning deceiver as its ideal of virtue. But it will be objected that, logically unassailable as this position may be, it is contradicted by facts. Over-production, the disproportion between the productivity of labour and the capacity for consumption as conditioned by the existing social institutions, has practically existed for generations; and yet it would be a gross exaggeration to assert that the moral sensibilities of civilised humanity had undergone such a terrible degeneration as is indicated above. It is certainly true that, in consequence of the increasingly reckless industrial competitive struggle, many kinds of valueless articles are produced in larger and larger quantities--nay, that there is beginning to prevail a certain confusion in public opinion, which is no longer able clearly to distinguish between honest services and successful roguery; but it is equally true, on the other hand, that never before was humanity in all its forms so highly esteemed and so widely diffused as it is in the present. These undeniable facts, however, do not show that over-production can ultimately lead to any other than the above-indicated results--which would be logical nonsense; they only show, on the one hand, that this dreadful morbid phenomenon in the industrial domain of mankind has not yet been long enough in existence to have fully matured its fruit, and that, on the other hand, the moral instinct of mankind felt a presentiment of the right way out of the economic dilemma long before that right way had become practicable. It is only a few generations since the disproportion between productivity and consumption became unmistakably evident. and what are a few generations in the life of mankind? The ethics of exploitation needed many centuries in order to subvert that of cannibalism: why should the relapse into the ethics of cannibalism proceed so much more rapidly? But the instinctive presentiment that growing civilisation will be connected, not with social stagnation and moral retrogression, but with both social and moral progress--this yearning for liberty, equality, and fraternity ineradicably implanted in the Western mind, despite all the follies and the horrors to which it for a time gave rise--it was just this 'drop of foreign blood in the European family of nations,' this Semitic-Christian leaven, which, when the time of servitude was past, preserved that Western mind from falling even temporarily into a servile and barbarous decay. Things will *not* follow the last indicated course of evolution--exploitation will *not* persist alongside of increased productivity; and that is the reason why the indicated moral consequences will not ensue. If, however, it be assumed that material progress and exploitation combined are the future lot of mankind, this cannot logically be conceived otherwise than as accompanied by a complete moral relapse. Yet a third form of evolution may be assumed as conceivable: in the antagonism between the productivity of labour and the current social rights, the former--the new form of labour--might succumb; in the face of the impossibility of making full use of the acquired industrial capacity, mankind might lose this capacity again. In such a case, the concord between productivity and consumption, labour and right, would have recovered the old basis, and as a consequence the ethics of mankind might also remain in the same track. Progress towards genuine philanthropy would necessarily be suspended, for the struggle for existence would, as before, be based upon the subjugation of one's fellow-men, but the necessity for the struggle of annihilation would be avoided. The presentiment of the possibility of such a development was not foreign to the Western mind; there have not been wanting, particularly during the last generations, attempts, partly conscious and partly unconscious, to load men's minds in this direction. Alarmed and driven nearly to distraction by the strangling embrace of over-production, whole nations have at times attacked the fundamental sources of production, sought to choke the springs of the fruitfulness of labour, and persecuted with violent hatred the progress of civilisation, whose fruits were for the time so bitter. These attacks upon popular culture, upon the different kinds of division of labour, upon machinery, cannot be understood except in connection with the occasional attempts to end the discord between production and distribution by diminishing the former. It is impossible not to see that in this way morality also would be preserved from a degeneracy the real cause of which this sort of reformers certainly did not understand, but which hovered before their mind's eye as an indistinct presentiment. And now, having noticed *seriatim* the three conceivable forms of evolution--namely, (1) the adaptation of social rights to the new and higher forms of labour and the corresponding evolution of a new and higher morality; (2) the permanent antagonism between the form of labour and social rights, and the corresponding degeneracy of morality; (3) the adaptation of the form of labour to the hitherto existing social rights by the sacrifice of the higher productivity, and the corresponding permanence of the hitherto existing morality--we now ask ourselves whether in the struggle between these three tendencies any but the first can come off as conqueror. They all three are conceivable; but is it conceivable that material or moral decay can assert itself by the side of both moral and material progress, or will ultimately triumph over these? It is possible, we will say even probable, that but for our successful undertaking begun twenty-five years ago, mankind would for the most part still longer have continued to traverse the path of moral degeneracy on the one hand, and of antagonism to progress on the other; yet there would never therefore have been altogether wanting attempts in the direction of social deliverance, and the ultimate triumph of such attempts could be only a question of time. No; mankind owes us nothing which it would not have obtained without us: if we claim to have rendered any service, it is merely that of having brought about more speedily, and perhaps with less bloodshed, that which must have come. [Vehement and long-continued applause and enthusiastic cheers from all sides. The leaders of the opposition one after another shook the hands of the speaker and assured him of their support.]

(End of Third Day's Debate)

CHAPTER XXVI

Fourth Day

The President (Dr. Strahl): We have reached the third point in the agenda: *Are not want and misery necessary conditions of existence; and would not over-population inevitably ensue were misery for a time to disappear from the earth?* I call upon Mr. Robert Murchison.

Robert Murchison (*Right*): I must first of all, in the name of myself and of those of my colleagues who entertained doubts of the practicability of the work of social reform, formally declare that we are now thoroughly convinced, not only of the practicability, but also of the inevitable accomplishment of that reform. Moreover, what has already been advanced has matured our hope that the other side will succeed in removing as completely the doubts that still cling to our minds. In the meantime I hold it to be my duty, in the interest of all, to seek explanations by strongly stating the grounds of such doubts as I am not yet able to free myself from. By far the most important of these doubts, one which has not yet been touched upon, is the subject now before us for discussion. It refers not to the practicability, but to the durability of the work of universal freedom and prosperity. Economic justice must and will become an accomplished fact: that we know. But have we a right to infer that it will permanently assert itself? Economic justice will be followed by wealth for all living. Want and misery, with their retinue of destructive vices, will disappear from the surface of the earth. But together with these will disappear those restraints which have hitherto kept in check the numerical growth of the human race. The population will increase more and more, until at last--though that day may be far off--the earth will not be able to support its inhabitants. I will not trouble you with a detailed repetition and justification of the well-known principle of my renowned countryman, Malthus. Much has been urged against that principle, but hitherto nothing of a convincing character. That the increase in a geometric ratio of the number of living individuals has no other natural check than that of a deficiency of food is a natural law to which not merely man but every living being is inexorably subject. Just as herrings, if they could freely multiply, would ultimately fill the whole of the ocean, so would man, if the increase of his numbers were not checked by the lack of food, inevitably leave no space unoccupied upon the surface of the globe.

This cruel truth is confirmed by the experience of all ages and of all nations; everywhere we see that it is lack of food, want with its consequences, that keeps the number of the living within certain limits; and it will remain so in all future times. Economic justice can very largely extend the area included in these sad limits, but can never altogether abolish the limits. Under its *régime* the food-supply can be increased tenfold, a hundredfold, but it cannot be increased indefinitely. And when the inevitable limit is reached, what then? Wealth will then gradually give place to privation and ultimately to extreme want; a want that is the more dreadful and hopeless because there will be no escape from its all-embracing curse--not even that partial escape which exploitation had formerly offered to a few. Will, then, mankind, after having passed from cannibalism to exploitation and from that to economic justice, revert to exploitation, perhaps even to cannibalism? Who can say? It seems evident that economic justice is not a phase of evolution which our race could enjoy for any great length of time. It is true that Malthus and others after him have proposed to substitute for the repressive law of misery certain preventives of over-population. But these preventives are all based upon artificial and systematic suppression of the increase of population. If they could be effectively employed at all, such an employment of them is conceivable only in a poor population groaning under the worst consequences of misery; I cannot imagine that men enjoying abundance and leisure, and in possession of the most perfect freedom, will subject themselves to sexual privations. In my opinion, this kind of prevention could not under the most favourable circumstances, come into play in a free society until the pressure of over-population had become very great, and the former prosperity, and with that perhaps the sense of individual liberty also, had been materially diminished. This is not a pleasant prospect, quite apart from the moral repulsiveness of all such violent interference with the relations of the sexes--relations which would be specially delicate under the *régime* of economic justice. The perspective shows us in the background a picture which contrasts sadly with the luxuriant promise of the beginning. Do the men of Freeland think that they are able to defend their creation from these dangers?

Franzisko Espero (*Left*): Man differs from other living beings in having to prepare food for himself, and, in fact, in being able, with increasing civilisation, to prepare it the more easily the denser the population becomes. Carey, an eminent American economist, has pointed this out, and has thereby shown that the otherwise indisputably operative natural law, according to which a species has an inevitable tendency to outgrow its means of sustenance, does not apply to man. The fact that want and misery have, notwithstanding, hitherto always operated as checks upon the growth of the population is not the result of a natural law but of exploitation. The earth would have produced enough for all if everyone had but been able to make free use of his powers. But, as we have seen, exploitation is an institution of men, not of nature. Get rid of that, and you have driven away the spectre of hunger for ever.

Stefan Való (*Freeland*): I think it will be well at once to state what is the Freeland attitude towards the subject now under discussion. The honourable member from Brazil (Espero) is correct in connecting the actual misery of mankind--in the epoch of exploitation--with human institutions instead of with the operation of natural forces. The masses suffered want because they were kept in servitude, not because the earth was incapable of yielding more copious supplies. I will add that this actual misery never prevented the masses from multiplying up to the point at which the further increase of population was checked by other factors--nay, that as a rule misery acted as a stimulus to the increase of the population. Our friend from Brazil is in error, however, when, relying upon the empty rhetoric of Carey, he denies that the growth of the population, if it could go on indefinitely, would necessarily at last lead to a lack of food. The first of the speakers of to-day has rightly remarked that in such a case the time must come when there would no longer be space enough on the earth for the men who were born. But can we conceive the condition possible in which our race should cover the surface of the earth like a plague of locusts? Nay, a really unlimited and continuous increase in the number of human beings would not merely ultimately cover the whole surface of the earth, but would exhaust the material necessary for the crowded masses of human bodies. The growth of the population *must*, therefore, have some limit, and so far are Malthus and his followers correct. Whether this limit is to be found exactly in the supply of food is another question--a question which cannot be satisfactorily answered in the affirmative until it has been positively shown, or at any rate rendered plausible, that other factors do not come into play long before a lack of food is felt--factors whose operation is such that the limit of necessary food-supply is never, except in very rare cases, even approximately reached, to say nothing of its being crossed.

Arthur French (*Right*): What I have just heard fills me with astonishment. The member of the Freeland government admits--what certainly cannot reasonably be denied--that unlimited growth of population is an impossibility; and yet he denies that a lack of food is the sought-for check of over-population. It may be at once admitted that Malthus was in error in supposing that this natural check had already been operative in human society. Men have suffered hunger because they were prevented from supplying themselves with food, not because the earth was incapable of copiously--or, at least, more copiously--nourishing them all. Exploitation has therefore proved to be a check upon over-population operating before the limit of necessary food has been reached; it has been a kind of hunger-cure which man has applied to himself before nature had condemned him to suffer hunger. I am less able to understand what the speaker means when he says the misery artificially produced by exploitation has sometimes proved to be, not a check, but rather a stimulus to the growth of population. But I should particularly like to hear more about those other factors which are alleged to have acted as effective checks, and which the speaker evidently anticipates will in future regulate the growth of the population. These factors are to produce the wonderful effect of preventing the population from ever getting even approximately near to the limit of the necessary food-supply. They cannot be artificial and arbitrarily applied means, otherwise a member of the Freeland government, of this commonwealth based upon absolute freedom, would not speak of them so confidently. But apart from all this, how can there be any doubt of the operation of such an elementary factor of restriction as the lack of food in human society, whilst it is to be seen so conspicuously throughout the whole of organic nature? Is man alone among living beings exempt from the operation of this law of nature; or do the Freelanders perhaps know of some means that would compel, say, the herrings so to control their number as not to approach the limit of their food-supplies, or, rather, induce them to preserve such a reasonable rate of increase as would be most conducive to the prosperous continuance of their species?

This cutting apostrophe produced a great sensation. The tension of expectancy was still further increased when several members of the Freeland government--including Stefan Való, who had already spoken--urgently begged the President to take part in the debate. The whole assembly seemed conscious that the discussion--not merely the special one of the day, but the general discussion of the congress--had reached its decisive point. If the advocates of economic justice were able successfully to meet the objections now urged by their opponents, and to show that those objections were groundless, then the great argumentative battle was won. What would follow would not concern the question *whether*, but merely the question *how*, the new social order could be well and lastingly established. But if the Freeland evidence failed upon this point--if the structure of Opposition argumentation could not in this case be blown down like a house of cards--then all the previous successes of the advocates of economic justice would count for nothing. To remove the misery of the present merely to prepare the way for a more hopeless misery in the future, was not that which had aroused men's enthusiasm. If there remained only a shadow of such a danger, the death-knell of economic justice had been sounded.

Amid breathless silence, Dr. Strahl rose to speak, after he had given up the chair to his colleague Ney, of the Freeland government.

Our friend of the Right (he began) ended his appeal to us with the question whether we in Freeland knew of any means which would compel the herrings to confine the increase in their numbers within such bounds as would best conduce to the prosperous continuance of their species. My answer is brief and to the point: Yes, we know of such a means. [Sensation.] You are astonished? You need not be, dear friends, for you know of it as well as we do; and what leads you to think you do not know of it is merely that peculiar mental shortsightedness which prevents men from perceiving the application of well-known facts to any subject upon which the prejudices they have drunk in with their mother's milk prevent them making a right use of their senses and their judgment. So I assert that you all know of the means in question as well as we do. But I do not say, as you seem to assume, that either you or we were in a position to teach this prudence to the herrings--a task, in fact, which would be scarcely practicable. I assert, rather, that our common knowledge of the means in question is derived not from our gift of invention, but from our gift of observation--in other words, that the herrings have always acted in the way in which, according to the opinion of the propounder of the question, they need to be taught how to act by our wisdom; and that, therefore, in order to attain to a knowledge of the mode of action in question, we need merely first, open our eyes and see *what* goes on in nature, and secondly, make some use of our understanding in order that we may find out the *how* of this natural procedure.

Let us, then, first open our eyes--that is, let us remove the bandages with which inherited economic prejudices have blinded us. To make this the easier, my friends, I ask you to fix your mind upon any living thing-- the herring, for example--without thinking of any possible reference which it may have to the question of population in human society. Do not seek among the herrings for any explanation of human misery, but regard them simply as one of the many kinds of boarders at the table of nature. It will then be impossible for you not to perceive that, though this species of animal is represented by very many individuals, yet those individuals are not too numerous to find places at nature's table. Nay, I assert that--always supposing you keep merely the herring in mind, and are not at the same time looking at human misery in the background--you would think it absurd to suppose for a moment that the herrings, if they were more numerous than they are, would not find food enough in the ocean--that there were just as many of them as could be fully fed at the table of nature. Or let us take another species of animal, the relations between which and its food-supply we are not obliged to arrive at by reflection, but, if necessary, could easily discover by actual observation--namely, the elephant. Malthus calculated how long it would take for a pair of elephants to fill the world with their descendants, and concluded that it would be lack of food which would ultimately check their indefinite increase. Does not the most superficial glance show you that nowhere on the earth are there nearly so many elephants as would find nourishment in abundance? Would you not think anyone a dotard who would try to convince you of the contrary? Thus you all know--and I wish first of all to make sure of this--that every kind of animal, whether rare or common, more or less fruitful, regularly keeps within such limits as to its numerical increase as are far, infinitely far, removed from a deficiency in the supply of food. I go further: you not merely know that this is so--you know also that it must be so, and why it must be so. Careful observation of natural events teaches you that a species which regularly increased to the very limit of the food-supply, and was, therefore, regularly exposed to hunger and privations, must necessarily degenerate--nay, you cannot fail to see that to many kinds of animals such an increase to the limit of the food-supply would mean sudden destruction. For the animals sow not, neither do they reap; they do not store up provisions for the satisfaction of future needs: and if at any time they were obliged to consume all the food that nature had produced for them, they would thereby, as a rule, destroy the source of their future food-supply, and would not merely suffer hunger, but would all starve. You know, therefore, that that inexhaustible abundance which, in contrast to the misery of human society, everywhere prevails in nature, and which, because of this contrast, the thinkers and poets of all ages have spoken and sung about, is not due to accident, but to necessity; and it only remains now to discover that natural process, that causal connection, by virtue of which this state of things necessarily exists. Upon this point men were treated to nothing but vague phrases when Malthus lived. The veil which hid the history of the evolution of the organic world had not then been lifted; men were therefore obliged to content themselves with explaining all that took place in the kingdoms of animals and plants as the work of Providence or of the so-called vital force--which naturally even then prevented no one from seeing and understanding the fact as well as the necessity of this formerly inexplicable natural phenomenon. But you, living in the century of Darwin, cannot for a moment entertain any doubt upon this last point. You know that it is through the struggle for existence that the living beings have developed into what they are--that properties which prove to be useful and essential to the well-being of a species are called forth, perfected, and fixed by this struggle; and, on the other hand, properties which prove to be detrimental to the well-being of a species are suppressed and removed. Now, since the property of never increasing to the limit of the food-supply is not only advantageous but absolutely necessary to the well-being--nay, to the existence--of every species, it must have been called forth, perfected, and fixed as a permanent specific character by the struggle for existence. You knew all this, my friends, before I said it; but this knowledge was so consciously present to your mind as to be of use in the process of thinking only when purely botanical or zoological questions were under consideration: as soon as in your organ of thought the strings of social or economic problems were struck, there fell a thick, opaque veil over this knowledge which was so clear before. The world no longer appeared to you as it is, but as it looks through the said veil of acquired prejudices and false notions; and your judgment no longer obeyed those universal laws which, under the name of 'logic,' in other cases compelled your respect, but indulged in singular capers which--if the said veil had not fallen over your senses--could not have failed to make you laugh. Indeed, so accustomed have you become to mistake the pictures which this veil shows to you for the actual world that you are not able to free yourselves from them even after you have roused yourselves to tear the veil in pieces. The false notions and erroneous conclusions of the Malthusian theory arose from the fact that its author was not able to discover the true source of the misery of mankind. He asked himself why did the Irish peasant and the Egyptian fellah suffer hunger? He was prevented by the above-mentioned veil from seeing that they suffered hunger because the produce of their labour was taken away from them--because, in fact, they were not permitted to labour. But he perceived that the masses everywhere and always suffered hunger--in some places and at some times less severely than in other places and at other times: yet, in spite of all their painful toil and industry, they perpetually suffered hunger, and had done so from time immemorial. Hence he at last came to the conclusion that this universal hungering was a consequence of a natural law. He further concluded that the fellah and the Irish peasant and the peoples of all parts of the world and of all times had suffered and still suffer hunger because there are too many of them; and there are too many of them because it is only hunger that prevents them from becoming still more numerous. That the world, perplexed by the enigma of misery, should believe *this* becomes intelligible when one reflects that misery must have a cause, and erroneous explanations must obtain credence when right ones are wanting. But it is remarkable, my friends, that you, who have recognised in exploitation and servitude the causes of misery, should still believe in that strange natural law which Malthus invented for the purpose of constructing out of it the above-mentioned makeshift. This means that, though you have torn the veil in pieces, your mind and your senses are still enveloped in its tatters. You have released yourselves sufficiently to see why the fellah and the Irish peasant suffer hunger to-day, but you tremble in fear that our posterity will have to endure the horrors of over-population. You still see the herring threatened with starvation, and the elephant wandering with an empty stomach over the bare-eaten forest-lands of Hindostan and Africa; and you pass in thought from the herring and the elephant to our poor over-populated posterity.

Tremendous applause burst forth from all parts of the hall when Dr. Strahl had finished. As he passed from the speaker's tribune to the President's chair, he was cordially shaken by the hand, not only by his friends who crowded around him, but also by the leaders of the Opposition, who gladly and unreservedly acknowledged themselves convinced. The excitement was so great that it was some time before the debate could be resumed. At last the President obtained a hearing for one of the previous speakers.

Robert Murchison (*Right*): I rise for the second time, on behalf of those who sit near me, first to declare that we are fully and definitively convinced. You will readily believe that we do not regret our defeat, but are honestly and heartily glad of it. Who would not be glad to discover that a dreadful figure which filled him with terror and alarm was nothing but a scarecrow? And even a sense of shame has been spared us by the magnanimity of the leader of the opposite party, who laid emphasis upon the fact that not merely we, but even his adherents outside of Freeland, still cherished in their hearts the same foolish anxiety, begotten of acquired and hereditary prejudices and false notions. The phantoms fled before his clear words, our laughter follows them as they flee, and we now breathe freely. But, if we might still rely upon the magnanimity of the happy dwellers in Freeland, the after-effects of the anxiety we have endured still linger in us. We are like children who have been happily talked out of our foolish dread of the 'black man,' but who nevertheless do not like to be left alone in the dark. We would beg you to let your light shine into a few dark corners out of which we cannot clearly see our way. Do not despise us if we still secretly believe a little in the black man. We will not forget that he is merely a bugbear; but it will pacify us to hear from your own mouths what the true and natural facts of the case are. In the first place, what are, in your opinion, the means employed by nature, in the struggle for the existence of species, to keep the growth of numbers from reaching the limit of the food-supply? Understand, we ask this time merely for an expression of opinion--of course, you cannot, any more than anyone else, *know* certainly how this has been done and is being done in individual cases; and if your answer should happen to be simply, 'We have formed no definite opinion upon the subject,' we should not on that account entertain any doubt whatever as to the self-evident truth that every living being possesses the characteristic in question, and that the origin of that characteristic must be sought somewhere in the struggle for existence. In order to be convinced that the stag has acquired his fleetness, the lion his strength, the fox his cunning, in the struggle for existence, it is not necessary for us to know exactly how this has come about; yet it is well to hear the opinions as to such subjects of men who have evidently thought much about them. Therefore we ask for your opinions on the question of the power of adaptation in fecundity.

Lothar Wallace (*Freeland*): We think that the characteristic in question, as it is common to all organisms, must have been acquired in a very early stage of evolution of the organic world; from which it follows that we are scarcely able to form definite conceptions of the details of the struggle for existence of those times--as, for example, of the process of evolution to which the stag owes his swiftness. We can only say in general that between fecundity and the death-rate an equilibrium must have been established through the agency of the mode of living. A species threatened with extinction would increase its fecundity or (by changing its habits) diminish its death-rate; whilst, on the other hand, a species threatened with a too rapid increase would diminish its fecundity or (again by changing its habits) increase its death-rate. Naturally the death-rate in question is not supposed to depend upon merely sickness and old age, but to be due in part to external dangers. The great fecundity, for example, of the heiring would, according to this view, be both cause and effect of its habits of life, which exposed it in its migrations to enormous destruction. Whether the herring and other migratory fishes adopted their present habits because of their exceptional fecundity--the origin of which would then have to be sought in some other natural cause--or whether those habits were originally due to some other cause, and provoked their exceptional fecundity, we cannot tell. But that a relation of action and reaction exists and must necessarily exist here is evident, since a species whose death-rate is increased by an increase of danger must die out if this increase of death-rate is not accompanied by an increased fecundity; and, in the same way, increased fecundity, when not followed by an increased death-rate, must in a short time lead to deterioration. At any rate, it can be shown that, whether deterioration or extermination has been the agent, species have died out; and it can be inferred thence that some species do not possess this power of effecting an equilibrium between fecundity and death-rate. But this conclusion would be too hasty a one. All natural processes of adaptation take place very gradually; and if a violent change in external relations suddenly produces a very considerable increase in the death-rate, it may be that the species cannot adapt its fecundity to the new circumstances rapidly enough to save itself from destruction. To infer thence that the species in question did not possess this power of adaptation at all would be as great a mistake as it would be to argue that, for example, because the stag, or the lion, or the fox, notwithstanding their fleetness, strength, or cunning, are not protected from extermination in the face of overpowering dangers, therefore these beasts do not possess swiftness, strength, or cunning, or that these properties of theirs are not the outcome of an adaptation to dangers called forth in the struggle for existence.

Since there can be no doubt that the power of adaptation, of which we have just spoken, was absolutely necessary to the perpetuation of any species in the struggle for existence in the very beginning of organic life upon our planet, it must have been acquired in immemorial antiquity, and must consequently be a part of the ancient heritage of all existing organisms. There certainly was a time, in the very beginning of life, when this power of adaptation was not yet acquired; but nature has an infallible means of making not only useful but necessary characters the common property of posterity, and this means is the extirpation of species incapable of such a power of adaptation. The selection in the struggle for existence is effected by the preservation of those only who are capable of development and of transmitting their acquired characters to posterity until those characters become fixed, such individuals as revert to the former condition being exterminated as they appear.

The reciprocal adaptation of fecundity to death-rate has thus belonged unquestionably for a long time to the specific character of all existing species without exception. Its presence is manifested not merely in the great universal fact that all species, despite many varying dangers--leaving out of view sudden external catastrophes and attacks of special violence--are preserved from either extermination or deterioration, but also in isolated phenomena which afford a more intimate glimpse into the physiological processes upon which the adaptation in question depends. Human knowledge does not yet extend very far in this direction, but accident and investigation have already given us a few hints. Thus, for example, we know that, as a rule, high feeding diminishes the fecundity of animals; stallions, bulls, etc., must not become fat or their procreative power is lessened, and the same has been observed in a number of female animals. As to man, it has long been observed that the poor are more fruitful than the rich, and, as a rule, notwithstanding the much greater mortality of their children, bring up larger families. The word 'proletarian' is derived from this phenomenon as it was known to the Romans; in England, Switzerland, and in several other countries the upper classes--that is, the rich--living in ease and abundance, have relatively fewer children--nay, to a great extent decrease in numbers. The census statistics in civilised countries show a general inverse ratio between national wealth and the growth of the population--a fact which, however, will be misinterpreted unless one carefully avoids confounding the wealth of certain classes in a nation with the average level of prosperity, which alone has to be taken into account here. In Europe, Russia takes the lead in the rate of growth of population, and is without question in one sense the poorest country in Europe. France stands lowest, the country which for more than a century has exhibited the most equable distribution of prosperity. That the English population increases more rapidly, though the total wealth of England is at least equal to that of France, is explained by the unequal distribution of its wealth. Moreover, it is not merely wealth that influences the growth of population--the ways in which the wealth is employed appear to have something to do with it. In the United States of America, for example, we find--apart from immigration--a large increase with an average high degree of prosperity, offering thus an apparent exception to our rule. Yet if we bear in mind the national character of the Yankees, excitable and incapable of calm enjoyment, the exception is sufficiently explained, and it is brought into harmony with the above principle. But the study of this subject is still in its infancy, and we cannot expect to see it clearly in its whole complex; nevertheless the facts already known show that the connection between the habits and life of fecundity is universally operative.

John Vuketich (*Right*): Certain phenomena connected with variations in population appear, however, to contradict the principles that disastrous circumstances act as stimuli to fecundity. For example, the fact that the number of births suddenly increases after a war or an epidemic, in short when the population has been decimated by any calamity, is to be explained by the sudden increase in the relative food-supply on account of the diminution of the number of the people. In this case, the greater facility of supplying one's wants produces a result which our theory teaches us to expect from a greater difficulty in doing so.

Jan Velden (*Right*): I know that this is the customary explanation of the well-known phenomenon just mentioned, and I must admit that an hour ago I should have accepted this explanation as plausible. Now, however, I do not hesitate to pronounce it absurd. Or can we really allow it to be maintained that, after a war or an epidemic, it is easier to get a living, wealth is greater, than before these misfortunes? I think that generally the contrary is the fact; after wars and epidemics men are more miserable than before, and on that account, and not because it is easier to get a living, their fecundity increases.

The conception to which our friend has just appealed is exactly like that concerning the famishing herrings or elephants; it has been entertained only because economic prejudice was in want of it, and it prevails only so far as this prejudice still requires it. If we were not now discussing the population question, but were speaking merely of war and peace, disease and health, the previous speaker would certainly regard me with astonishment, would indeed think me beside myself, if I were to be guilty of the absurdity of contending that, for example, after the Thirty Years' War the decimated remains of the German nation enjoyed greater prosperity and found it easier to live, or that the survivors of the great plagues of antiquity and the Middle Ages were better off than was the case before the plagues. His sound judgment would at once reject this singular notion; and if I showed myself to be obstinate, he could speedily refute me out of the old chronicles which describe in such vivid colours the fearful misery of those times. But since it is the population question which is under consideration, and some of the shreds of that veil of which our honoured President spoke seem to flutter before his eyes, he heedlessly mistakes the absurdity in question for a self-evident truth which does not even ask for closer examination. The misery that follows war and disease now becomes--and is treated as if it must be so, as if it cannot be imagined otherwise--a condition in which it is easier to obtain a supply of food, since--thus will the veil of orthodoxy have it--misery is produced only by over-population. Since men suffer want because they are too numerous, it *must* be better for them when they have been decimated by war and disease. From this categorical 'must' there is no appeal, either to the sound judgment of men, or to the best known facts; and should rebellious reason nevertheless venture to appeal, something is found wherewith to silence her too loud voice, as for example the reminder that the survivors would find their wealth increased by what they inherited from the dead, that the supply of hands--the demand is simply conveniently forgotten in this connection--has been lessened, and so on.

Edmond Renauld (*Centre*): I wish to draw attention to another method of violently bringing the fact that the growth of the population bears an inverse ratio to the national prosperity into harmony with the Malthusian theory of population, or at least of weakening the antagonism to this theory. For example, in order to explain the fact that the French people, 'in spite of their greater average well-being,' increase more slowly than many poorer nations, the calumny is spread abroad that the blame attaches to artificial prevention, the so-called 'two-children system.' Even in France many believe in this myth, because they--ensnared by Malthus's false population law--are not able to explain the fact differently. Yet this two-children system is a foolish fable, so far as the nation, and not merely a relatively small section of the nation, is concerned. It is true that in France there are more families with few children than there are in other countries; but this is very easily explained by the fact that the French, on account of their greater average prosperity, are on the whole less fruitful than most other peoples. But that the Frenchman intentionally limits his children to two is an absurdity that can be believed only by the bitter adherents of a theory which, finding itself contradicted by facts, distorts and moulds the facts in order to make them harmonise with itself. It should not be overlooked that such a limitation would mean, where it was exercised, not a slow increase, but a tolerably rapid extinction. Nothing, absolutely nothing, exists to prove that French parents exercise an arbitrary systematic restraint; the irregularity of chance is as conspicuous here as in any other country, with only the general exception that large families are rarer and small ones more frequent than elsewhere, a fact which, as has been said, is due to diminished fecundity and not to any 'system' whatever.

At the same time, I do not deny that the wealthy classes, particularly where the bringing up of children is exceedingly costly, do to some extent indulge in objectionable preventive practices, which, however, are said to be not altogether unknown in other countries.

Albert Molnár (*Centre*): The just mentioned fable of the two-children system is also prevalent among certain races living in Hungary, particularly among the Germans of Transylvania and among the inhabitants of certain Magyar districts on the Theiss. The truth here also is, that--apart, of course, from a few exceptions--the cause of the small increase in population must be sought in a lower degree of fecundity, which fecundity--and I would particularly emphasise this--everywhere in Hungary bears an inverse proportion to the prosperity of the people. The slaves of the mountainous north, who live in the deepest poverty, and the Roumanians of Transylvania, who vegetate in a like miserable condition, are all very prolific. Notwithstanding centuries of continuous absorption by the neighbouring German and Magyar elements, these races still multiply faster than the Germans and the Magyars. The Germans, living in more comfortable circumstances, and the few Magyars of the northern palatinate, are far less prolific, yet they multiply with tolerable rapidity. The Germans and Magyars of the plains, in possession of considerable wealth, are almost stationary, as are the already mentioned Saxons of Transylvania.

Robert Murchison (*Right*): In the second place, we would ask whether, contrary to the former assumption that man in his character of natural organism was subject to a universal law of nature imposing no check upon increase in numbers but that of deficiency of food--we would ask whether, on the contrary, the power acquired by man over other creatures does not constitute him an exception to that now correctly stated law of nature which provides that an equilibrium between fecundity and death-rate shall automatically establish itself before a lack of food is experienced. Our misgiving is strengthened by the fact that among other animals, as a rule, it is not so much the change that occurs in the fecundity of the species, as that which occurs in the relation of the species to external foes, that restores the equilibrium when the death-rate has been altered by any cause. Let us assume, for example, the herrings have lost a very dangerous foe--say that man, for some reason or other, has ceased to catch them--it is probable that their indefinite increase will not in the first instance be checked by a change in their fecundity, but an actual large increase in the number of the herrings will most likely lead to such an increase in the number and activity of their other natural foes that an equilibrium will again be brought about by that means.

Man, as lord of the creation, especially civilised man, has generally no other foe but himself to fear. Here, then, when the death-rate happens to be diminished by the disappearance of evils which he had brought upon himself, the equilibrium could be restored *only* by a diminution of fecundity; here it would be as if nature was prevented from employing that other expedient which, in the world of lower animals, she, as a rule, resorts to at once, the increase of the death-rate by new dangers. I admit that several facts mentioned by the last speaker belonging to the Freeland government show that nature would find this, her only remaining expedient--the spontaneous diminution of fecundity--quite sufficient. It cannot be denied that the number of births decreases with increasing prosperity; but is it certain that this will take place to a sufficient extent permanently and radically to avert any danger whatever of over-population? For, apart from very rare exceptions which tire too insignificant to make a rule in such an important matter, the births have everywhere a little exceeded the deaths, though the latter have hitherto been everywhere unnaturally increased by misery, crime, and unwholesome habits of life; and if in future it remains the rule that the births preponderate, let us say to only a very small extent, then eventually, though not perhaps for many thousands of years, over-population must occur, for the lack of any external check.

In order permanently to prevent this, there must be established sooner or later an absolute equilibrium between births and deaths. Can we really depend upon nature spontaneously to guarantee us this? Is it absolutely certain that nature will, as it were, say to man: 'My child, you have by the exercise of your reason emancipated yourself from my control in many points. You have made ineffectual and inapplicable all but one of those means by which I protected your animal kindred from excessive increase, and the one means you have left untouched is just that which I have been accustomed to employ only in extreme cases. Do not look to me alone to furnish you with effectual protection against that evil, but make use of your reason for that purpose--*for that also is my gift.'*

The supposition that, in this matter, nature really indicates that man is to exercise some kind of self-help gains weight when one recalls the course of human evolution. Our Freeland friends have very appositely and strikingly shown us how the men of the two former epochs of civilisation treated each other, first as beasts for slaughter and then as beasts of burden. And what was it but want that drove them to both of these courses? Is not the conviction forced upon us that our ancestors were compelled at first to eat each other, and, when they refrained from that, to decimate each other, simply because they had become too strong to be saved from over-population by the interposition of nature? In the first epoch of civilisation man protected himself against a scarcity of food by slaying and, driven by hunger, straightway devouring, his competitor at nature's table. What happened in the second epoch of civilisation was essentially the same: men were consumed slowly, by piecemeal, and a check put upon their increase by killing them and their offspring slowly through the pains and miseries of servitude. In short, since man has learnt to use his reason he has ceased to be a purely natural creature, his own will has become partly responsible for his fate; and it seems to me that in the population question of the future he will not be left to the operation of nature alone, but must learn how to help himself.

Lothar Montfort (*Freeland*): That man, by the exercise of his reason, has made himself king of nature, and has no special need to fear any foe but himself, is certainly true; and it is just as true that he can and ought to use this reason of his in all the relations of the struggle for existence. Moreover, I do not doubt that if it were really true, as the previous speaker apprehended, that man has become too strong for nature to save him from over-population in the same way in which she saved his lower fellow-creatures, then man would be perfectly able to solve this problem by a right use of his own reason. Should he actually be threatened by over-population after he had left off persecuting his fellow men, recourse could and would be had to the voluntary restriction of the number of children.

In the first place, it is not too much to expect that physiology would be able to supply us with means which, while they were effectual, would not be injurious to health or obnoxious to the aesthetic sentiment, and would involve the exercise of no ascetic continence; though all the means hitherto offered from different quarters, and here and there actually employed, fail to meet at least one or more of these conditions. In the second place, it is certain that public opinion would be in favour of prevention as soon as prevention was really demanded in the public interest. That the declamations of the apostles of prevention, powerful as they have been, have not succeeded in winning over the sympathies of the people is due to the fact that those apostles have been demanding what was altogether superfluous. There has hitherto been, and there is now, no over-population; the working classes would not be in the least benefited by refraining from the begetting of children; hence, prevention would in truth have been nothing but a kind of offering up of children to the Moloch of exploitational prejudice. The popular instinct has not allowed itself to be deceived, and moral views are determined by the moral instincts, not by theories. On the other hand, if there were a real threat of over-population, in whatever form, the restriction of the number of births would then be a matter of general interest, and the public views upon prevention would necessarily change. Should such a change occur, it would be quite within the power of society to regulate the growth of population according to the needs of the time. It may safely be assumed that no interference on the part of the authorities will be called for; the exercise of compulsion by the authorities is absolutely foreign to the free society, and cannot be taken into consideration at all. The modern opinion concerning the population question, the opinion that is gradually acquiring the force of a moral principle--viz. that it is reprehensible to beget a large number of children--must prove itself to be sufficiently powerful for the purpose, it being taken for granted, of course, that means of prevention were available which were absolutely trustworthy, and did not sin against the aesthetic sentiment. But if this did not suffice, the incentive to restriction would be furnished by the increased cost of bringing up children, or by some other circumstance.

But it is really superfluous to go into these considerations, for in this matter nature has no need whatever of the conscious assistance of man. Man is, in this respect, no exception; what he expects from nature has been given in the same degree to other creatures, and all that is essential has already been furnished to him.

As to the first point, I need merely remark that, though man is the king of animals, he is in no way different from all the others as to the point under consideration. There are animals which, when the danger from one foe diminishes, may be exposed to increased danger from other foes, and in the case of such, therefore, as the previous speaker quite correctly said, the restoration of the disturbed equilibrium does not necessarily presuppose a diminution of fecundity. But there are other animals which, in this matter, are exactly in the same position as man. They have no foes at all whom they need fear, and a change of death-rate among them can therefore be compensated for only by a corresponding change in the power of propagation. The great beasts of prey of the desert and the sea, as well as many other animals, belong to this category. What foe prevents lions and tigers, sperm-whales, and sharks from multiplying until they reach the limit of their food supply? Does man prevent them? If anyone is really in doubt as to this, I would ask who prevented them in those unnumbered thousands of years in which man was not able to vie with them, or did not yet exist? But they have never--as species--suffered from lack of food; consequently nature must have furnished to them exactly what *we* expect from her.

In fact, as I have said, she has already furnished us with it. For it is not correct that, in the earlier epochs of civilisation, man assisted nature in maintaining the requisite equilibrium between the death-rate and the fecundity of his species. It is true that men assisted in increasing their own death-rate by slaying each other, and by torturing each other to death; but they did not in this way restore an equilibrium that had been disturbed by too great fecundity or too low a mortality; on the contrary, they disturbed an equilibrium already established by nature, and compelled nature to make good by increased fecundity the losses occasioned by the brutal interference of man. The previous speaker is in error when he ascribes the rise of anthropophagy in the first competitive struggles in human society to hunger, to the limitation of the food supply, by which the savages were driven to kill, and eventually to eat, their fellow savages. Whether the opponent was killed or not made no material difference in the relations between these two-legged beasts of prey and their food supply. Nature herself took care that they never increased to the actual limit of their food supply; if they had been ten times more numerous they would have found the food in their woods to be neither more nor less abundant. They opposed and murdered each other out of ill-will and hatred, impelled not by actual want but by the claim which each one made to everything (without knowing how to be mutually helpful in acquiring what all longed for, as is the case under the *régime* of economic justice). Whether there were many or few of them is a matter of indifference. Put two tribes of ten men each upon a given piece of land, and they will persecute each other as fiercely as if each tribe consisted of thousands. It is true that the popular imagination generally associates cannibalism with a lack of food or of flesh; but this mistake is possible only because the doctrine of exploitation fills the minds of its adherents with the hallucination of over-population. Certainly cannibals do not possess abundance in the sense in which civilised men do, but this is because they are savages who have not, or have scarcely, risen out of the first stage of human development. To suppose that they were driven into cannibalism by over-population and the lack of food, is to exhibit a singular carelessness in reasoning. For it is never the hungry who indulge in human flesh, but those who have plenty, the rich; human flesh is not an article of food to the cannibal, but a dainty morsel, and this horrible taste is always a secondary phenomenon; the cannibal acquires a taste for a practice which originally sprang from nothing but his hatred of his enemy.

Again, neither is the action of the exploiter induced by a diminution of the food supply, nor would such a diminution prevent future over-population. Men resort to mutual oppression, not because food is scarcer, but because it is more abundant, and more easily obtainable than before; and the misery which is thereby occasioned to the oppressed does not diminish but increases their number. It is true that misery at the same time decimates those unfortunates whose fecundity it continually increases; but experience shows that the latter process exceeds the former, otherwise the population could not increase the more rapidly the more proletarian the condition of the people became, and become the more stationary the higher the relative prosperity of the people rose.

That, apart from insignificant exceptions, an actually stationary condition has never been known is easily explained from the fact that actual prosperity, real social well-being, has never yet been attained. When once this becomes an accomplished fact the perfect equilibrium will not be long in establishing itself. The same applies to every part of nature in virtue of a great law that dominates all living creatures; and there is nothing to justify the assumption that man alone among all his fellow-creatures is *not* under the domination of that law.

(*End of Fourth Day's Debate*)

CHAPTER XXVII

Fifth Day

The fourth point in the Agenda was: *Is it possible to introduce the institutions of economic justice everywhere without prejudice to inherited rights and vested interests; and, if possible, what are the proper means of doing this?*

Ernst Wolmut (*belonging to no party*) opened the debate: I do not think it necessary to lay stress upon the fact that the discussion of the subject now before us cannot and ought not materially to influence our convictions. Whether it be everywhere possible or not to protect vested interests will hinder no one from adopting the principle of economic justice, and that at once and with all possible energy. We are not likely to be prevented from according a full share of justice to the immense majority of our working fellow-men by a fear lest the exploiting classes should suffer, any more than the promoters of the railroads were stayed in their work by the knowledge that carriers or the innkeepers on the old highways would suffer. It is, however, both necessary and useful to state the case clearly, and as speedily as possible to show to those who are threatened with inevitable loss what will be the extent of the sacrifice they will have to make. For I take it to be a matter of course that such a sacrifice is inevitable. No one suffered anything through the establishment of the Freeland commonwealth; but this was because there were here no inherited rights or vested interests to be interfered with. There were no landlords, no capitalists, no employers to be reckoned with. It is different with us in the Old World. What is to be done with our wealthy classes, and how shall we settle all the questions concerning the land, the capital, and the labour over which the wealthy now have complete control? Will it not be humane, and therefore also prudent, to make some compensation to those who will be deprived of their possessions? Will not the new order work better if this small sacrifice is made, and embittered foes are thereby converted into grateful friends?

Alonso Campeador (*Extreme Left*): I would earnestly warn you against such pusillanimous sentimentality, which would not win over the foes of the new order, but would only supply them with the means of attacking it, or shall we say allow them to retain those means. If we would exercise justice towards them, we should give to them, as to all other men, an opportunity of making a profitable use of their powers. They cannot or will not labour. They are accustomed to take their ease while others labour for them. Does this constitute a just claim to exceptional treatment? But it will be objected that they ask for only what belongs to them, nay, only a part of what belongs to them. Very well. But what right have they to this so-called property? Have they cultivated the ground to which they lay claim? Is the capital which they use the fruit of *their* labour? Does the human labour-force which carries on their undertakings belong to them? No; no one has a natural right to more than the produce of his own labour; and since in the new order of things this principle deprives no one of anything, but, on the contrary, leads to the greatest possible degree of productiveness, no one has any ground for complaint--that is to say, no one who is content with what is his own and does not covet what rightly belongs to some one else. To acknowledge the claims of those who covet what is not theirs would be like acknowledging the claims of the robber or thief to the property he has stolen.

It will be said that owners possess what they have *bonâ fide*; their claim is based upon laws hitherto universally respected. Right. Therefore we do not *punish* these *bonâ fide* possessors; we simply take from them what they can no longer possess *bonâ fide*. But the owners have paid the full value for what they must now give up: why should they lose their purchase-money, seeing that the purchase was authorised by the law then in force? Is the new law to have a retrospective force? These are among the questions we hear. But no one need be staggered by these questions unless he pleases. For the purchase-money rightly belonged to the possessor of it as little as the thing purchased; he who buys stolen goods with stolen money has no claim for compensation. If he acts in good faith he is not obnoxious to punishment-- but entitled to compensation?

Yet--and this is the last triumph of the faint-hearted--the purchase-money, that is, the capital sunk in land or in any business, can be legally the property of the possessor even in our sense of the term. The possessor may have produced it by his own labour and saved it: is he not in that case entitled to compensation? Yes, certainly; in this case, to refuse compensation for such capital would be robbery; but is not the establishment of economic justice, which gives a right to the produce of any kind of future labour, a fully adequate compensation for that capital which has really been produced by the possessor's own labour? Consider how poorly a man's own labour was remunerated under the exploiting system of industry, what capital could be saved out of what was really one's own labour, and you will not then say that a real worker who possessed any such savings will not find a sufficient compensation in the ten-fold or hundred-fold increase of the produce of his labour. But perhaps a difficulty is found in the possibility that this small capitalist might no longer be capable of work? Granted; and provision is made for this in the new order of things. The honest worker receives his maintenance allowance when his strength has left him; even he will have no occasion to sigh for what he had saved in the exploiting times of the past. To these maintenance allowances I refer also those other exploiters whose habits have robbed them of both desire and ability to work. The free community of the future will be magnanimous enough not to let them suffer want; even they have, as our fellow-men, this claim upon the new order; but any right beyond this I deny.

Stanislaus Llowski (*Freeland*): We in Freeland take a different standpoint. The exploiting world could, without being false to itself, forcibly override acquired rights in order to carry out what might be the order of the day; it could--and has almost always done so--carry into force any new law based upon the sword, without troubling itself about the claims of the vanquished; it could do all this because force and oppression were its proper foundation. Its motto was, 'Mine is what I can take and keep'; therefore he who took what another no longer had the power to keep acted in perfect accordance with his right, whether he could base his claim upon the fortune of war or upon a parliamentary majority. If we recognised this ancient right, matters would be very simple: we have become the stronger and can take what we please. The hypocrisy of the modern so-called international law, which has a horror of brutal confiscations, need not stand in our way any more than it has ever stood in the way of anyone who had power. Conquerors no longer deprived the conquered of their land, they no longer plundered or made men their slaves; but in truth, it was only in appearance that these practices had ceased: it was only the form, not the essence of the thing, that had changed. The victor retained his right of legislating for the vanquished; and the earnings of the vanquished were more effectually than ever transferred to the pockets of the victors in the forms of all kinds of taxes, of restrictions, and rights of sovereignty. 'Property' was 'sacred,' not even that of the subjugated was touched; merely the fruits of property were taken by the strong. This we, too, could do. Take the property from its owners? How brutal; what a mockery of the sacred rights of property! But to raise the taxes until they swallowed up the whole of the property--who in the exploiting world would be able to say *that* was contrary to justice? Yet we declare it to be so, for we recognise no right to treat the minority of possessors differently from the minority of workers; and as in our eyes property is sacred, we must respect it when it belongs to the wealthy classes as much as when it belongs to ourselves.

But--objects the member on the Left--the victorious majority make no claim of right of private property in the land and in the productive capital.

Certainly; but they do not possess anything which they will have to renounce in the future, while the minority does; hence to dispossess the possessors in favour of those who did not possess, in order that equality of right might prevail in future, would not be to treat both alike.

But--and this is the weightiest argument in the eyes of our friend--the minority is said to have at present no valid title to their property; they owe it to exploitation, and we do not recognise this as a just title; exploitation is robbery, and he who has stolen, though he did it in good faith, possesses no claim to compensation. This reasoning is also false. Exploitation is robbery only in an economic, not in a juridical, sense; it was not merely *considered* to be permissible--it *was* so. The exploiter did not act illegally though in good faith; rather he acted legally when in his day he exploited; and acted legally not merely on the formal ground that the law, as it then existed, allowed him thus to act, but because he could not act otherwise. This appropriation of other men's earnings, which, in an economic sense, we are compelled, and rightly so, to call robbery, was--let us not forget that--the necessary condition of any really productive highly organised labour whatever, so long as the workers were not able to freely organise and discipline themselves. Economic robbery, the relation of master held by the few towards the many, constituted an effective economic service that had the strongest right to claim the profit of other men's labour, which was in fact rendered profitable by it. Subsequently to confiscate the thus acquired compensation for the services rendered, because such services had become superfluous or indeed detrimental, would in truth be robbery, not merely in an economic sense, but in a legal sense--an offence against the principles of economic justice.

Then are those who have been exploiters to retain undiminished the fruit of their 'economic robbery'? Yes; but two things must be noted. In all ages it has been held to be the right of the community to dispossess owners of certain kinds of property without committing any offence against the sacredness of property, provided full compensation was offered to the owners. In the abolition of slavery, of serfdom, of certain burdens on the land, and the like, no one has ever found anything that was reprehensible, provided the owner of the slaves or of the land was compensated to the full value of the property taken from him. In the second place, it is to be noted that the community is bound to guarantee to the owners their property, but not the profit which has hitherto been obtained from it.

If you apply these two principles to the acquired rights which the Free Society found existing, you will find that, while the land is taken from the landowners, the value of it must be paid; the Society has nothing to do with movable capital, and the same holds good of the profit which the employers have hitherto drawn from their relation to the workers. The Society can also claim the right of obtaining possession of the movable productive property, so far as it may appear to be to the public interest to do this. Such an interest does not here come in question, for, apart from the fact that movable means of production can be created in any quantity that is required, there is no reason to fear that the owners will hold back theirs when they find what is both the only and the absolutely best employment for it in dealing with the associated workers. But, in the future, capitalists will not receive interest for their property, or, if they do, it will be only temporarily. There is as little occasion as there is right to forbid the receiving of interest; but, as every borrower will be able to get capital without interest, the paying of interest will cease automatically. Just as little can or need the Free Society forbid the former employers to hire workers to labour for them for stipulated wages; such workers will no longer be found.

Ali Ben Safi (*Right*): Where is the Free Commonwealth to obtain the means to purchase all the land, and at the same time to furnish the workers with business capital? It is possible that some rich countries may be able to accomplish this by straining all their resources; but how could we in Persia find the £125,000,000, at which the fixed property was estimated at the last assessment, to say nothing of the hitherto totally lacking business capital?

François Renaud (*Right*): On the contrary, I fear that the--from a legal standpoint certainly unassailable--justice to the former owners will occasion the greatest difficulties to just the richest countries. Their greater means involve the heavier claims upon those means; for in proportion as those countries are really richer will the value of the land be higher, and the workers, because more skilful in carrying on highly developed capitalistic methods of industry, will at once require larger amounts of business capital, which the community will have to furnish. So far, then, the greater strength and the heavier burden balance each other. But to this it must be added that in the more advanced countries the amount of mobile capital requiring compensation is far greater than that of poor countries. As interest is to cease, all these numberless invested milliards then bearing interest will be withdrawn: whence will the means be suddenly obtained promptly to meet all these calls?

Clark (*Freeland*): The last two speakers entertain unnecessary fears. The sums required to get possession of the land, to pay back the circulating capital, and to furnish the workers with more abundant means for carrying on business, are certainly enormous--are at any rate larger than the material advance of any country whatever can even approximately supply quickly enough to place the country in a position to bear such burdens in their full extent. Certainly, if the transition to economic justice were followed immediately by its full results--if, for example, such transition lifted any country at once to that degree of wealth which we enjoy in Freeland-- comparatively little difficulty would be experienced in responding to the heavy demands that would be made; but this condition would not be reached for years; the tasks you must undertake would be more than you could perform, if you had at once to discharge the whole of your responsibilities. But you have no reason whatever to fear this. Simply because interest will cease will neither landowner nor capitalist have any motive for insisting upon immediate payment, but will be quite content to accept payment in such instalments as shall suit the convenience of the community or the private debtors--should there be any such--and which could be easily accommodated to the interests of those who were entitled to receive the payment. When it is considered that the latter would be compelled either to let their capital lie idle or to consume it, it will appear evident that, if only the slightest advantage were offered them, they would prefer to receive their property in instalments, so far as they did not actually want to use it themselves.

You have quite as little reason to fear the demand which will be made for supplying the workers with the means of carrying on business. If your exploited masses already possessed the ability to make use of all those highly developed capitalistic implements of industry which we employ in Freeland, then certainly the Old World would have to renounce any attempt even approximately to meet at once the enormous demand for capital which would be made upon it. In such a case the milliard and a-half of souls who would pass over to the new order of things would require two billions of pounds; but the two milliards of men will not require these two billions, because they would not know what to do with the enormous produce of the labour called forth by such means of production. To dispose of so much produce it would be necessary for every family in the five divisions of the globe to possess the art of consuming a minimum of from £600 to £700 per year, as our Freeland families do; and, believe us, dear friends, your masses, just escaped from the servitude of many thousands of years, at present entirely lack this art. You will not produce more than can be consumed. You have not been able to do so yet, and will certainly not be able to do it when the consumption of the workers is able to supply the only reason for production. The extent and the intensity of production have been and remain the determining factors in the extent and kind of the means of production. You will at any time be able to create what you are able to make use of; and if here and there the demand grow somewhat more rapidly than can be conveniently met out of the surplus acquired by the continually increasing productiveness of labour, you must for a time be content to suffer inconvenience--that is, you must temporarily forego the gratification of some of your newly acquired wants in order the more rapidly to develop your labour in the future.

For the rest, I can only repeat that the Freeland commonwealth will always be prepared, in its own interests, to place its means at your disposal, so far as they will go. We calculate that your wealth--that is, looking at the subject from the standpoint of *our* material interests, your ability to purchase those commodities which we have special natural facilities for producing, and your power of producing those commodities which we can take in exchange for ours with the greatest advantage to you--will, in the course of the next two or three years, at least double, and probably treble and quadruple. From this we promise ourselves a yearly increase of about a milliard pounds sterling in our Freeland income. We have determined to apply this increase for a time, not to the extension of our consumption and of our own investments, but to place it at your disposal, as we have already done the unemployed surplus of our insurance reserve fund, and to continue to do this as long as it may seem necessary. [Tremendous applause.]

The President: I believe I am expressing the wish of the assembly when I ask William Stuart, the special representative of the American Congress, who arrived at Eden Vale this morning, to state to us the proposals laid before the congress of his country by the committee entrusted with the drawing up of the scheme for adopting the *régime* of economic equality of rights.

William Stuart: In the name of the representatives of the American people, I ask the kind attention of this distinguished assembly, and particularly of the representatives of Freeland who are present, to a series of legislative enactments which it is proposed to make for the purpose of carrying us--with the energy by which we are characterised, and, at the same time, without injury to existing interests--out of the economic conditions that have hitherto existed into those of economic equality of rights. Our government found themselves obliged to take this step because our nation is the first outside of Freeland--at least, so far as we are aware--which has passed the stage of discussion, and is about immediately to take action and carry out the work. The institutions of economic justice are no longer novelties; we can follow a well-proved precedent, the example of Freeland, and we intend to follow that example, with a few unessential modifications rendered necessary by the special characteristics of the American country and people. On the other hand, we lack experience; and as, notwithstanding our well-known 'go-ahead' habits, we would rather have advice before than after undertaking so important a task, I am sent to ask your opinion and report it to the American Congress before the recommendations of the committee have become law.

It is proposed to declare all the land in the United States to be ownerless, but to pay all the present owners the full assessed value. In order to meet the cases of those who may think they have not received a sufficient compensation, special commissions of duly qualified persons will be appointed for the hearing of all appeals, and the public opinion of the States is prepared to support these commissions in treating all claims with the utmost consideration. It is proposed to deal with buildings in the same way, with the proviso that dwelling-houses occupied by the owners may be excepted at the owners' wish. The purchase-money shall be paid forthwith or by instalments, according to the wish of the seller, with the proviso that for every year over which the payment of the instalment shall be extended a premium of one fifth per cent. shall be given, to be paid to the seller in the form of an additional instalment after the whole of the original purchase-money has been paid. The payment is not to extend over more than fifty years. Suppose a property be valued at ten thousand dollars; then the owner, if he wishes to have the whole sum at once, receives his ten thousand, with which he can do what he pleases; but if he prefers, for example, to receive it in ten yearly instalments of 1,000 dollars, he has a right to ten premiums of 20 dollars each, which will be paid to him in a lump sum of 200 dollars as an eleventh instalment. If he wishes the payment to be in fifty instalments of 200 dollars, then his premiums will amount to fifty times twenty dollars--that is, to 1,000 dollars--which will be paid in five further instalments of 200 dollars. The national debt is to be paid off in the same way.

The existing debit and credit relations of private individuals remain intact, except that the debtor shall have the right of immediate repayment of the borrowed capital, whatever may have been the terms originally agreed upon. As the commonwealth will be prepared to furnish capital for any kind of production whatever, the private debtor will be in a position to exercise the right above-mentioned; but, according to the proposal of the committee, the commonwealth shall, for the present, demand of its debtors the same premium which it guarantees to its creditors. The object of this regulation is obvious: it is to prevent the private creditors--in case no advantage accrues to them--from withdrawing their capital from business and locking it up. If those who needed capital had their needs at first supplied without cost, simply upon undertaking gradually to repay the borrowed capital, they would not be disposed to make any compensatory arrangement with their former creditors, whilst, should the committee's proposal be adopted, they would be willing to pay to those creditors the same premiums as they would have to pay to the commonwealth.

The opinions of the committee were at first divided as to the amount of the premiums to be guaranteed and demanded. A minority was in favour of fixing a maximum of one in a thousand for each year of delayed payment: they thought that would be sufficient to induce most of the capitalists to place in the hands of the commonwealth or of private producers the property which otherwise they must at once consume or allow to lie idle. Eventually, however, the minority came over to the view of the majority, who preferred to fix the maximum higher than was necessary, rather than by untimely parsimony expose the commonwealth to the danger of seeing the capital withdrawn which could be so profitably used in the equipment of production. The voting was influenced by the consideration that we, as the first, outside of Freeland, among whom capital would receive no interest, must be prepared, if only temporarily, to stand against the disturbing influences of foreign capital. That such disturbing influences have not been felt in Freeland, though here no premium of any kind has ever been in force, whilst interest has been paid everywhere else in the world, was an example not applicable to our case, as we have not to decide--as you in Freeland have--what to do with capital which we do *not* need, and which, after all conceivable demands on capital have been met, still remains disposable; but, on the other hand, we have to attract and to retain capital of which we have urgent need. But that the proposed one-fifth per cent. will suffice for this purpose we are able with certainty to infer from the double circumstance that, in the first place, the anticipated adoption of this proposal, which naturally became known at once to our world of capitalists, has produced a decided tendency homewards of our capital invested abroad. It is evident, therefore, that capitalists scarcely expect to get elsewhere more for large amounts of capital than we intend to offer. In the second place, the capitalistic transactions which have recently been concluded or are in contemplation show that our home capital is already changing hands at a rate of interest corresponding to our proposed premium. Anyone in the United States who to-day seeks for a loan gets readily what he wants at one-fifth per cent., particularly if he wishes to borrow for a long period. Such seekers of capital among us at present are, of course, in most cases companies already formed or in process of formation.

Thanks to the fact that the election for the Constituent Congress has been the means of universally diffusing the intelligence that it was intended to act upon the principle of respecting most scrupulously all acquired rights, productive activity during the period of transition has suffered no disturbance, but has rather received a fresh impetus. The companies in process of formation compel the existing undertakers to make a considerable rise in wages in order to retain the labour requisite for the provisional carrying on of their concerns; and as this rise in wages has suddenly increased the demand for all kinds of production it has become still more the interest of the undertakers to guard against any interruption in their production. These two tendencies mutually strengthen each other to such a degree that at the present time the minimum wages exceed three dollars a day, and a feverish spirit of enterprise has taken possession of the whole business world. The machine industry, in particular, exhibits an activity that makes all former notions upon the subject appear ridiculous. The dread of over-production has become a myth, and since the undertakers can reckon upon finding very soon in the associations willing purchasers of well-organised concerns, they do not refrain from making the fullest possible use of the last moments left of their private activity. Even the landlords find their advantage in this, for the value of land has naturally risen very materially in consequence of the rapidly grown demand for all kinds of the produce of land. In short, everything justifies us in anticipating that the transition to the new order of things with us will take place not only easily and smoothly, but also in a way most gratifying to *all* classes of our people.

The President asked the assembly whether they would continue the debate on the fourth point on the Agenda, by at once discussing the message from the American Congress; or whether they would first receive the report which the Freeland commissioner in Russia had sent by a messenger who had just arrived in Eden Vale. As the congress decided to hear the report,

Demeter Novikof (messenger of the Freeland commissioner for Russia) said: When we, the commissioners appointed by the Freeland central government at the wish of the Russian people, arrived in Moscow, we found quiet--at least externally--so far restored that the parties which had been attacking each other with reckless fury had agreed to a provisional truce at the news of our arrival. Not merely the cannons and rifles, but even the guillotine and the gallows were at rest. Radoslajev, our plenipotentiary commissioner, called the chiefs of the parties together, induced them to lay down their weapons, to give up their prisoners, to dissolve the seven different parliaments, each one of which had been assuming the authority of exclusive representative of the Russian people; and then, after he had furnished himself for the interim with a council of reliable men belonging to the different parties, he made arrangements for the election of a constituent assembly with all possible speed.

As production and trade were nearly at a standstill, the misery was boundless. To be an employer was looked upon by several of the extreme parties as a crime worthy of death; hence no one dared to give workers anything to do. In most parts of the empire the ignorant masses, who had been held down in slavish obedience, were altogether incapable of organising themselves; and as the most extreme of the Nihilists had begun to guillotine the organisers of the free associations as 'masters in disguise,' it seemed almost as if mutual slaughter could henceforth be the only occupation that would be pursued in Russia.

The proclamation, in which Radoslajev called upon the people to elect an assembly, and in which he insisted upon the security of the person and of property as *conditio sine quâ non* of our continued assistance, calmed the minds of the people, but it did not suffice to produce a speedy growth of productive activity. When, therefore, the constituent assembly met, Radoslajev proposed a mixed system as transition stage into the *régime* of economic justice. In this mixed system a kind of transitory Communism was to be combined with the germs of the Free Society and with certain remnants of the old industrial system.

In the first place, however, order had to be restored in the existing legal relationships. During the reign of terror previous to our arrival, all fixed possessions were declared to be the property of the nation, without giving any compensation to the former owners. All existing debts were simply cancelled; and the first business now was to make good as far as practicable the injury done by these acts of violence. But at first the new national assembly showed itself to be intractable upon these points. Hatred of the old order was so universal and so strong that even those who had been dispossessed did not venture to endorse our views. The private property of the epoch of exploitation was considered to be merely robbery and theft, the claims for compensation were so obnoxious to many that a deputation of former landowners and manufacturers, headed by two who had borne the title of grand-duke, conjured Radoslajev to desist from his purpose, lest the scarcely sleeping nihilistic fanaticism should be awaked anew. The latter, nevertheless, persisted in his demands, after he had consulted us Freelanders who had been appointed to assist him. He announced to the national assembly that we were far from wishing to force our views upon the Russian nation, but that, on the other hand, Russia could not require us to take part in a work based--in our eyes--upon robbery; and this threat, backed by our withdrawal, finally had its effect. The national assembly made another attempt to evade the task of passing a measure which it disliked: it offered Radoslajev the dictatorship during the period of transition. After he had refused this offer, the assembly gave in and reluctantly proceeded with the consideration of the compensation law. Radoslajev drafted a bill according to which the former owners were to be paid the full value in instalments; and the old relations between the debtors and creditors were to be restored, and the debts discharged in full also in instalments. However, Radoslajev could not get this bill passed unaltered. The national assembly unanimously voted a clause to the effect that no one claim for compensation should exceed 100,000 rubles; if debts were owing to the owner, the amount was to be added, yet no claim for compensation for debts owing to any one creditor was to exceed 100,000 rubles. For property that had been devastated or destroyed a similar maximum of compensation was voted.

In the meantime we had made all the necessary arrangements for organising production upon the new principles. Private undertakers did not venture to come forward, though the field was left open to them; on the other hand, free associations of workers, after the pattern of those in Freeland, were soon organised, particularly in the western governments of Russia. The great mass of the working population, however, proved to be as yet incapable of organising themselves, and the government was therefore compelled to come to their assistance. Twenty responsible committees were appointed for twenty different branches of production, and these committees, with the help of such local intelligence as they found at their disposal, took the work of production in hand. The liberty of the people was so far respected that no one was compelled to engage in any particular kind of work; but those who took part in the work organised by the authorities had to conform to all the directions of the latter. At present there are 83,000 such undertakings at work, with twelve and a-half millions of workers. The division of the profits in these associations is made according to a system derived in part from the principles of free association and in part from those of Communism. One half of the net profits is equally divided among the whole twelve and a-half millions of workers; the other half is divided by each undertaking among its own workers. In this way, we hope on the one hand to secure every undertaking from the worst consequences of any accidental miscarriage in its production, and on the other to arouse the interest of the workers in the success of each individual undertaking. The managers of these productive corporations are paid according to the same mixed system.

The time of labour is fixed at thirty-six hours per week. Every worker is forced to undergo two hours' instruction daily, which instruction is at present given by 65,000 itinerant teachers, the number of whom is being continually increased. This obligation to learn ceases when certain examinations are passed. Down to the present time, 120,000 people's libraries have been established, to furnish which with the most needful books a number of large printing works have been set up in Russia, and the aid of the more important foreign printing establishments has also been called in; the Freeland printing works alone have already supplied twenty-eight million volumes. And as the teaching of children is being carried on with all conceivable energy--780 teachers' seminaries either have been or are about to be established; large numbers of teachers, &c., have been brought in from other Slav countries, particularly Bohemia--we hope to see the general level of popular culture so much raised in the course of a few years that the communistic element may be got rid of.

In the meantime, the control provisionally exercised over the masses who willingly submit to it will be utilised in the elevation and ennoblement of their habits and needs. Spirituous liquors, notably brandy, are given out in only limited quantities; on the other hand, care is taken that breweries are erected everywhere. The workers receive a part of their earnings in the form of good clothing; the wretched mud huts and dens in which the workmen live are being gradually superseded by neat family dwellings with small gardens. At least once a month the authorities appoint a public festival, when it is sought to raise the aesthetic taste of the participators by means of simple but good music, dramatic performances and popular addresses, and to cultivate their material taste by viands fit for rational and civilised beings. Special care is devoted to the education of the women. Nearly 80,000 itinerant women-teachers are now moving about the country, teaching the women--who are freed from all coarse kinds of labour--the elements of science as well as a more civilised style of household economy. These teachers also seek to increase the self-respect and elevate the tastes of the women, to enlighten them as to their new rights and duties, and particularly to remove the hitherto prevalent domestic brutality. As these apostles of a higher womanhood--as well as all the teachers--are supported by the full authority of the government, and devote themselves to their tasks with self-denying assiduity, very considerable results of their work are already visible. The wives of the working classes, who have hitherto been dirty, ill-treated, mulish beasts of burden, begin to show a sense of their dignity as human beings and as women. They no longer submit to be flogged by their husbands; they keep the latter, themselves, and their children clean and tidy; and emulate one another in acquiring useful knowledge. Thanks to the maintenance allowance for women, which was at once introduced, an incredible progress--nay, a veritable revolution--has taken place in the morals of the people. Whilst formerly, particularly among the urban proletariate, sexual licence and public prostitution were so generally prevalent that--as our Russian friends assure us--anyone might accost the first poorly clad girl he met in the streets without anticipating refusal, now sexual false steps are seldom heard of. Moreover, it is particularly interesting to observe the difference which public opinion makes between such offenders in the past and those of the present. Whilst the mantle of oblivion is thrown over the former, public opinion has no indulgence for the latter. 'The woman who sold herself in former times was an unfortunate; she who does it now is an abandoned woman,' say the people. The woman who in former times was a prostitute but is now blameless carries her head high, and looks down with haughty contempt upon the girl or the wife who, 'now that we women are no longer compelled to sell ourselves for bread,' commits the least offence.

(End of Fifth Day's Debate)

CHAPTER XXVIII

Sixth Day

The business begins with the continuation of the debate upon point 4 of the Agenda.

Ibrahim El Melek (*Right*): The very instructive reports from America and Russia, heard yesterday, afford strong proof that the transition to the system of economic justice is accomplished not merely the more easily, but also the more pleasantly for the wealthy classes, the more cultured and advanced the working classes are. In view of this, it will cause no wonder that we in Egypt do not expect to effect the change of system without painful convulsions. The nearness of Freeland, with the consequently speedy advent of its commissioners, who were received by the violently excited fellaheen with almost divine honours, has preserved us from scenes of cruel violence such as afflicted Russia for weeks. No murders and very little destruction of property have taken place; but the Egyptian national assembly, called into being by the Freeland Commissioners, shows itself far less inclined than its Russian contemporary to respect the compensation claims of the former owners. In this I see the ruling of fate, against which nothing can be done, and to which we must therefore submit with resignation. But I would exculpate from blame those who have had to suffer so severely. Though no one has expressly said it, yet I have an impression that the majority of the assembly are convinced that those who have composed the ruling classes are now everywhere suffering the lot which they have prepared for themselves. As to this, I would ask whether the landlords, capitalists, and employers of America, Australia, and Western Europe were less reckless in taking advantage of their position than those of Russia or Egypt? That they could not so easily do what they pleased with their working classes as the latter could is due to the greater energy of the American national character and to the greater power of resistance possessed by the masses, and not to the kindly disposition of the masters. Hence I cannot think it just that the Russian boyar or the Egyptian bey should lose his property, whilst the American speculator, the French capitalist, or the English lord should even derive profit from the revolution.

Lionel Spencer (*Centre*): The previous speaker may be correct in supposing that the wealthy classes of England, like those of America, will come out of the impending revolution without direct loss. There cannot be the slightest doubt that in England, as well as in France and in several other countries in which the government has had a democratic character, nothing will be taken from the wealthy classes for which they will not be fully compensated. But I am not able to see in this the play of blind fate. Observe that the sacrifices involved in the social revolution everywhere stand in an inverse ratio to what has hitherto been the rate of wages, which is the chief factor in determining the average level of popular culture. Where the masses have languished in brutish misery, no one can be surprised that, when they broke their chains, they should hurl themselves upon their oppressors with brutish fury. Again, the rate of wages is everywhere dependent upon the measure of political and social freedom which the wealthy classes grant to the masses. The Russian boyar or the Egyptian bey may be personally as kindly disposed as the American speculator or the English landlord; the essential difference lies in the fact that in America and England the fate of the masses was less dependent upon the personal behaviour of the wealthy classes than in Russia and Egypt. In the former countries, the wealthy classes--even if perhaps less kindly in their personal intercourse--were politically more discreet, more temperate than in the latter countries, and it is the fruit of this political discretion that they are now reaping. It may be that they knew themselves to be simply compelled to exercise this discretion: they exercised it, and what they did, and not their intentions, decided the result. Those that were the ruling classes in the backward countries are now atoning for the excessive exercise of their rights of mastership; they are now paying the difference between the wages they formerly gave and the--meagre enough- -general average of wages under the exploiting system.

Tei Fu (*Right*): The previous speaker overlooks the fact that the rate of wages depends, rot upon the will of the employer, but upon supply and demand. That the receiver of a hunger-wage has been degraded to a beast is unfortunately too true, and the massacres with which the masses of my fatherland, driven to desperation, everywhere introduced the work of emancipation are, like the events in Russia, eloquent proofs of this fact. But how could any political discretion on the part of the ruling classes have prevented this? The labour market in China was over-crowded, the supply of hands was too great for any power on earth to raise the wages.

Alexander Ming-Li (*Freeland*): My brother, Tei Fu, thinks that wages depend upon supply and demand. This is not an axiom that was thought out in our common fatherland, but one borrowed from the political economy of the West, but which, in a certain sense, is none the less correct on that account. It holds good of every commodity, consequently of human labour so long as that has to be offered for sale. But the price depends also upon two other things--namely, on the cost of production and the utility of the commodity: in fact, it is these two last-named factors that in the long run regulate the price, whilst the fluctuations of supply and demand can produce merely fluctuations within the limits fixed by the cost of production and the utility. In the long run as much must be paid for everything as its production costs; and in the long run no more can be obtained for a thing than its use is worth. All this has long been known, only unfortunately it has never been fully applied to the question of wages. What does the production of labour cost? Plainly, just so much as the means of life cost which will keep up the worker's strength. And what is the utility of human labour? Just as plainly, the value of what is produced by that human labour. What does this mean when applied to the labour market? Nothing else, it seems to me, than that the rate of wages--apart from the fluctuations due to supply and demand-- is in the long run determined by the habits of the worker on the one hand, and by the productiveness of his labour on the other. The first affects the demands of the workers, the second the terms granted by the employers.

But now, I beg my honoured fellow-countryman particularly to note what I am about to say. The habits of the masses are not unchangeable. Every human being naturally endeavours to live as comfortably as possible; and though it must be admitted that custom and habit will frequently for a time act restrictively upon this natural tendency to expansion in human wants, yet I can assert with a good conscience that our unhappy brethren in the Flowery Land did not go hungry and half-clad because of an invincible dislike to sufficient food and clothing, but that they would have been very glad to accustom themselves to more comfortable habits if only the paternal wisdom of all the Chinese governments had not always prevented it by most severely punishing all the attempts of the workers to agitate and to unite for the purpose of giving effect to their demands. Workers who united for such purposes were treated as rebels; and the wealthy classes of China- -this is their folly and their fault--have always given their approval to this criminal folly of the Chinese government.

I call this both folly and crime, because it not merely grossly offended against justice and humanity, but was also extremely detrimental to the interests of those who thus acted, and of those who approved of the action. As to the government, one would have thought that the insane and suicidal character of its action would long since have been recognised. A blind man could have seen that the government damaged its financial as well as its military strength in proportion as its measures against the lower classes were effective. The consumption by the masses has been in China, as in all other countries, the principal source of the national income, and the physical health of the people the basis of the military strength of the country. But whence could China derive duties and excise if the people were not able to consume anything; and how could its soldiery, recruited from the proletariate, exhibit courage and strength in the face of the enemy? This oppression of the masses was equally injurious to the interests of the wealthy classes. While the Chinese people consumed little they were not able to engage in the more highly productive forms of labour--that is, their labour had a wretchedly small utility because of the wretchedly small cost at which it was produced.

Thus the Chinese employer could pay but little for labour, because the worker was prevented from demanding much in such a way as would influence not merely the individual employer, but the labour market in general. The individual undertaker could have yielded to the demands of his workers to only a limited degree, since he as individual would have lost from his profits what he added to wages. But if wages had risen throughout the whole of China, this would have increased the demand to such a degree that Chinese labour would have become more productive-- that is, it would have been furnished with better means of production. The employers would have covered the rise in wages by the increased produce, not out of their profits; in fact, their profits would have grown--their wealth, represented by the capitalistic means of labour in their possession, would have increased. Of course this does not exclude the possibility that some branches of production might have suffered under this general change, for the increase of consumption resulting from better wages does not affect equally all articles in demand. It may be that while the average consumption has increased tenfold, the demand for a single commodity remains almost stationary--in fact, diminishes; but in this case it is certain that the demand for certain other commodities will increase more than ten-fold. The losses of individual employers are balanced by the proportionately larger profits of other employers; and it may be taken as a general rule that the wealth of the wealthy classes increases in exact proportion to the increase of wages which they are obliged to pay. It cannot be otherwise, for this wealth of the wealthy classes consists mainly of nothing else than the means of production which are used in the preparation of the commodities required by the whole nation.

Perhaps my honoured fellow countryman thinks that in the matter of rise of wages we move in a circle, inasmuch as on the one hand the productiveness of labour--that is, the utility of the power expended in labour--certainly cannot increase so long as the nation's consumption--that is, the amount which the labour power itself costs--does not increase, while on the other hand the latter increase is impossible until the former has taken place. If so, I would tell him that this is just the fatal superstition which the wealthy classes and the rulers of so many countries have now so cruelly to suffer for. Since, in the exploiting world, only a part, and as a rule a very small part, of the produce of labour went to wages, the employers--with very rare exceptions--were well able to grant a rise in wages even before the increase of produce had actually been obtained, and had resulted in a *universal* rise in wages. I would tell him that, especially in China, on the average even three or four times the wages would not have absorbed the whole profits--that is, of course, the old profits uninfluenced by the increase of produce. The employers *could* pay more, but they *would not*. From the standpoint of the individual this was quite intelligible; everyone seeks merely his own advantage, and this demands that one retains for one's self as large a part of any utility as possible, and hands over as little as possible to others. In this respect the American speculators, the French capitalists, and the English landlords, were not a grain better than our Chinese mandarins. But as a body the former acted differently from the latter. Notwithstanding the fact that the absurdity that wages *cannot* be raised was invented in the West and proclaimed from all the professorial chairs, the Western nations have for several generations been compelled by the more correct instinct of the people to act as if the contrary principles had been established. In theory they persisted in the teaching that wages could not be increased; in practice, however, they yielded more and more to the demands of the working masses, with whose undeniable successes the theory had to be accommodated as well as possible. You, my Chinese brethren, on the contrary, have in your policy adhered strictly to the teaching of this theory: you have first driven your toiling masses to desperation by making them feel that the State is their enemy; and you have then immediately taken advantage of every excess of which the despairing people have been guilty to impose 'order' in your sense of the word. Your hand was always lifted against the weaker: do not wonder that when they had become the stronger they avenged themselves by making you feel some small part of the sufferings they had endured.

This does not prevent us in Freeland--as our actions show--from condemning the violence that has been offered to those who formerly were oppressors, and from trying to make amends for it as well as we can. Hence we hold that the people of Russia, Egypt, and China--in short, everybody-- would do well to follow the example given by the United States of America. We think thus because this wise generosity is shown to be advantageous not merely for the wealthy classes, but also for the workers. Unfortunately it is not in our power at once to instil into the Russian muzhik, the Egyptian fellah, or the Chinese cooley such views as are natural to the workers of the advanced West. History is the final tribunal which will decree to everyone what he has deserved.

As no one else was down to speak on this point of the Agenda, the President closed the debate upon it, and opened that upon the fifth point:

Are economic justice and freedom the ultimate outcome of human evolution; and what will probably be the condition of mankind under such a régime?

Engelbert Wagner (*Right*): We are contemplating the inauguration of a new era of human development; want and crime will disappear from among men, and reason and philanthropy take possession of the throne which prejudice and brute force have hitherto occupied. But the apparent perfection of this condition appears to me to involve an essential contradiction to the first principle of the doctrine of human blessedness--namely, that man in order to be content needs discontent. In order to find a zest in enjoyment, this child of the dust must first suffer hunger; his possessions satiate him unless they are seasoned with longing and hope; his striving is paralysed unless he is inspired by unattained ideals. But what new ideal can henceforth hover before the mind of man--what can excite any further longing in him when abundance and leisure have been acquired for all? Is it not to be feared that, like Tannhaüser in the Venusberg, our descendants will pine for, and finally bring upon themselves, fresh bitternesses merely in order to escape the unchangeable monotony of the sweets of their existence? We are not made to bear unbroken good fortune; and an order of things that would procure such for us could therefore not last long. That the world if once emancipated from the fetters of servitude will again cast itself into them, that the old exploiting system shall ever return, is certainly not to be feared, according to what we have just heard; even a relapse into the material misery of the past through over-population is out of the question. But the more irrefragably the evidence of the impossibility of the return of any former kind of human unhappiness presses upon us, so much the more urgently is an answer demanded to the question: What will there be in the character of man's future destiny, what new ideals will arise, to prevent him from being swamped by a surfeit of happiness?

The President (Dr. Strahl): I take upon myself to answer this question from the chair, because I hope that what I am about to say will close the discussion upon the point of the Agenda now before us, and consequently the congress itself. From the nature of the subject we cannot expect any practical result to follow from the debate upon this last question, which was added to the Agenda merely because our foreign friends wished to learn, by way of conclusion to the previous discussions, what were our ideas as to the future. No mortal soul can have any definite ideas as to the future, for we can know only the past and the present. I venture to make only one positive assertion--namely, that the order of things which we propose to inaugurate will be in harmony with the general laws of evolution, as every foregoing human order has been; that it cannot be permanent and eternal; and that consequently it will by no means put an end to human striving and change and improvement. This holds good even with respect to the material conditions of mankind. In the future, as in the past, labour will be the price of enjoyment, and there is no reason to fear that in future the wish will lag behind the effort necessary to realise it. Thus mankind will not lack even the material stimulus to progress and to further striving. But man possesses intellectual as well as material needs, and the less imperative the latter become, so much the more widely and powerfully do the former make themselves felt. Intellectual hunger is a far more influential stimulus to effort than material hunger; and at present at least we are forced to believe that the former will never be appeased.

The fear that our race will sink into stagnation when the aims which have hitherto almost exclusively dominated its circle of ideas have been attained, is like the fancy of the child that the youth will give himself up to idleness as soon as he escapes the dread of the rod. It would be useless to attempt to make the child understand those other, and to him unknown, motives for activity by which the youth is influenced; and so we, standing now on the threshold of the youthful age of mankind and still half enslaved by the ideas of the childhood of our race, cannot know what new ideas mankind will conceive after the present ones have been realised. We can only say that they will be different, and presumably loftier ones. The new conditions of existence in which man will find himself in consequence of the introduction of economic freedom, will bring to maturity new properties, notions, and ideas, which no sagacity, no gift of mental construction possessed by anyone now living, is able to prefigure with accuracy. If, nevertheless, I venture to indicate some of the features of the future, I ask you not to attach to them any greater importance than you would to the fancies of a savage who, standing on the threshold leading from cannibalism to exploitation, might thousands of years ago have undertaken to form a conception of those changes which the invention of agriculture and of slavery would produce in the circumstances of his far-off successors. In this respect I have only one advantage over our remote ancestor: I know his history, while that of his ancestors was unknown to him. I can, therefore, seek counsel of the past in order to understand the future, while for him there was merely a present. I will now make use of this advantage; the course of human evolution in the past shall give us a few hints as to the significance of that phase of evolution into which we are now passing.

The original condition of mankind was freedom and peace in the animal sense--that is, freedom and peace among men, together with absolute dependence upon nature. The first great stage in evolution reached its climax when man turned against his fellow-men the weapon which had in the beginning been employed only in conflict with the world of beasts: dependence upon nature remained, but peace among men was broken.

The second stage in evolution is distinguished by the fact that man turns against nature, who had hitherto been his sovereign mistress, the intelligence which he had employed in mutually destructive warfare. He discovers the art of compelling nature to yield what she will not offer voluntarily--he produces. The chain by which the elements hold him bound is in this way loosened; but the first use which man makes of this gleam of deliverance from the bonds of merely animal servitude is to place fetters upon himself. The relaxing of dependence upon external nature and the alleviation of the conflict among men themselves--these are the acquisition of the second period.

The third stage of development begins with the dominion over nature gradually acquired by controlling the natural forces, and ends with the deliverance of mankind from the bonds of servitude. Independence of external control, freedom and peace among men, are its distinguishing features.

Here I would point out that the theatre of each of these phases of human progress has been a different one. The original home of our race was evidently the hottest part of the earth; under the tropics, in our struggles with the world of animals, we gained our first victories, and developed ourselves into warlike cannibals; but against the forces of nature, which reign supreme in that hot zone, we in our childhood could do nothing. Production, and afterwards slavery, could be carried on only outside of the tropics. On the other hand, it is quite as certain that man could not remove himself very far from the tropics so long as the productivity of his labour was still comparatively small, and he could not compel nature to furnish him with much more than she offered voluntarily. It is no mere accident that all civilisation began and first flourished exclusively in that zone which is equally removed from the equator and from the polar circle. In that temperate zone were found united all the conditions which protected the still infantile art of production from the danger of being crushed on the one hand or stunted on the other by the overwhelming power or the parsimony of nature. But this mean temperature, so favourable to the second phase of evolution, proved itself altogether unsuitable to the last step towards perfect control over nature. As human labour met with a generous reward, there was nothing to stimulate man's inventiveness to compel nature to serve man by her own, instead of by human, forces. This could happen only when the civilisation, which had acquired strength in the temperate zone, was transplanted into colder and less friendly regions, where human labour alone could no longer win from reluctant nature wealth enough to satisfy the claims of the ruling classes. Then first did necessity teach men how to employ the elemental forces in increasing the productiveness of human labour; the moderately cold zone is the birthplace of man's dominion over nature.

But when the third phase of evolution has found its close in economic justice, there will be, apparently, yet another change of scene. It might be said, if we cared to look for analogies, that this change of scene will be of a double character, corresponding to the double character of the change in institutions. The perfected control over nature will be seen in the fact that the whole earth, subjugated to man, has become man's own property; on the other hand, peace and freedom--which in themselves represent nothing new to mankind, but are as it were merely the return of the primitive relation of man to man--will find their analogies in the return to the primitive home of our race, the tropical world. That vigorous nature, which had formerly to be left lest civilisation should be killed in the very germ, can no longer be a hindrance, can only be a help to civilisation now that man, awaked to freedom, has attained to a full control over those forces which can be made serviceable to him. It will probably need several centuries before the civilised nations, whose northern wanderings and experiences have made them strangers in their birthplace, have afresh thoroughly acclimatised themselves here. In the meantime, the charming highlands which nature has placed--one might almost believe in anticipation of our attempt--directly under the equator, offer to the wanderers the desired dwelling-places, and, at any rate, the agriculture of the now commencing epoch of civilisation will have its headquarters here. Slowly but surely will man, who henceforth may freely choose his dwelling-place wherever productiveness and the charms of nature attract him, press towards the south, where merely to breathe and to behold is a delight beyond anything of the kind which the north has to offer. The notion that the torrid zone engenders stagnation of mind and body is a foolish fancy. There have been and there are strong and weak, vigorous and vigourless peoples in the north as well as in the south; and that civilisation has celebrated its highest triumphs under ice and snow is not due to anything in chilly temperatures essentially and permanently conducive to progress, but simply to the temporary requirements of the transition from the second to the third epoch of civilisation. In the future the centres of civilisation will have to be sought in proximity to the equator; while those countries which, during the last centuries--a short span of time--

have held up the banner of human progress will gradually lose their relative importance.

That man, having attained to control over the forces of nature and to undivided proprietorship of the whole planet, will ever actually take possession of and productively exploit the whole of the planet, is scarcely to be expected. In fact, past history almost tempts us to believe that the population of the earth has undergone scarcely any material change since civilisation began. Certainly, Europe to-day is several times more populous than it was thousands of years ago; and in America--putting out of sight the unquestionable extraordinary diminution in the population of Mexico and Peru--there has undeniably been a large increase in the number of inhabitants. Against all this we have to place the fact that large parts of Asia and Africa are at present almost uninhabited, though they formerly were the homes of untold millions. Thus, taking everything into consideration, the variations in population can never have exceeded a few hundred million souls. But assuming that the introduction of the new order of things, with its sudden and general diminution of the death-rate, will produce a revolution in this respect, that man's control over nature will be connected with a general increase in the number of the earth's masters, yet it may be considered as highly improbable that this increase will be particularly rapid, and that it will go on for any great length of time.

In one respect, certainly, there can and will be a sudden and considerable increase in the number of the living. In consequence of the greater longevity which will be the necessary result of rational habits of life, generations that have hitherto been consecutive will then be contemporaneous. In the exploiting world, on the average the father, worn out by misery, toil, and vice, died ere the son had reached maturity; in the future the parents will be buried by their great-grandchildren, and thus the number of the living will be speedily rained from a milliard and a-half to two milliards or to two and a-half, without any increase in human fecundity. But assuming that there be for a time an actual growth in population over and above that caused by this greater longevity, I hold it to be in the highest degree improbable that this growth can be a rapid one, and still less a continuous one. My opinion--based, it is true, upon analogy--is that a doubling of the population is the utmost we need reckon upon, so that the maximum population of the world may grow to five milliards. This number, very small in proportion to the size and productive capacity of our planet, will find abundant room and food in the most beautiful, most agreeable, and most fertile parts of the earth. Ninety-nine per cent. of the land superficies of the earth will be either not at all or very sparsely populated--so far as the population depends upon the production of the locality--and ninety per cent, will be cultivated either not at all or only to a very trifling extent.

That under the new order the earth will be transformed into a swarming ant-hill of thickly crowded inhabitants, that complete control over the elemental forces will lead to a destruction of all primitive natural fertility, there is therefore no reason whatever to fear. On the contrary, the more rationally distributed inhabitants will not crowd upon each other in the way in which they do at present in most civilised countries; and the greater fertility of the cultivated land of the future, in connection with the improved methods of cultivation, will make it possible to obtain from a smaller area a ten-fold greater supply for a double or a triple number of people than can be now obtained by the plough. The beauty and romance of nature are exposed to no danger whatever of being destroyed by the levelling instruments of future engineers; nay, it may be anticipated that a loving devotion to nature will be one of the chief pleasures of those future generations, who will treasure and guard in every natural wonder their inalienable and undivided property.

It is impossible to predict what course the development of material progress will take under the dominion of the new social principle. So much is evident, that the spirit of invention will apply itself far more than it has hitherto done to the task of finding out fresh methods of saving labour. This is a logical consequence of the fact that arrangements for the sparing of labour will now become profitable and applicable under all circumstances-- which has hitherto been the case only exceptionally. But it is probable that the future will surpass the present also in its comparative estimate of intellectual as more valuable than material progress. Hitherto the reverse has been the case: material wealth and material power have been the exclusive aims of human endeavour; intellectual culture has been at best prized merely as the means of attaining what was regarded as the real and final end. There have always been individuals who looked upon intellectual perfection as an end in itself; but there have always been isolated exceptions who have never been able to impress their character upon the whole race. The immense majority of men have been too ignorant and rude even to form a conception of purely intellectual endeavour; and the few who have been able to do so have been so absorbed in the reckless struggle for wealth and power, that they have found neither time nor attention for anything else. In fact, it lay in the essence of the exploiting system that under its dominion intellectual interests should be thrust into the background. In the mutual struggle for supremacy only those could succeed in becoming the hammer instead of the anvil who knew how to obtain control of material wealth; hence it was only these latter who could imprint their character upon the society they dominated, whilst the 'impractical,' who chased after intellectual aims, were forced down into the great subjugated herd. And the teaching of the history of civilisation compels us to admit that in the earlier epochs the chase after wealth could legitimately claim precedence over purely intellectual endeavour. It is true that intellectual perfection is the highest and final end of man; but as a certain amount of wealth is an indispensable condition of success in that highest sphere of effort, man must give to the acquisition of wealth his chief attention until that condition of higher progress is attained. That condition has now been attained, that amount of wealth has been acquired which makes the supply of the highest intellectual needs possible to all men; and there can be no doubt whatever that man will now awake to a consciousness of his proper destiny. That which he has hitherto striven after only incidentally, and, as it were, accidentally, will now become the object of his chief endeavour.

That this intellectual progress must produce a radical revolution in the sentiments and ideas of the coming generations is a matter of course. This holds good also of religious ideas. These have always been the faithful and necessary reflection of the contemporary conditions of human existence. In primitive times, so long as man carried on the struggle for existence only passively, like the beasts, he, like them, was without any religious conceptions. When he had taken the first step towards active engagement in the struggle for existence, and his dependence upon nature was to some extent weakened, but peace had not yet been broken with his fellow-men, he began to believe in helpful higher Powers that should fill his nets and drive the prey into his hands. When the war of annihilation broke out between man and man, then these higher Powers acquired a cruel and sanguinary character corresponding to the horribly altered form of the struggle for existence; the devil became the undisputed master of the world, which, regarded as thoroughly bad, was nevertheless worshipped as such. Next the struggle for supremacy superseded the struggle of annihilation; the first traces of humanity, consideration for the vanquished, showed itself, and in harmony with this the good gods were associated with the gods of evil, Ormuzd with Ahriman; and the more the horrors of cannibalism were forced into the background by the chivalrous virtues of the new lords of the world, the more pronounced became the authority of the good gods over the bad. But since it was the dominant classes who created the new faith, and since they needed for their prosperity the obedience of the subjugated, they naturally transplanted the principle of servitude into their heaven. The gods became severe, jealous masters; they demanded blind obedience, and punished with tyrannical cruelty every resistance to their will. This did not prevent the rulers from holding this to be the best of all worlds, despite its servitude and its vices; for to *them* servitude was well-pleasing, and as to the vices, they would be rid of the 'evil gods' if only the last remnant of resistance and disobedience--the only sources of all evil--were rooted out.

This kind of despotism was first attacked when the slaves found spokesmen. The most logical of these was Buddha, who, as he necessarily must from the standpoint of the slaves, again declared the world to be evil, and thence arrived at the only conclusion consistent with this assumption-- namely, that its non-existence, Nirvana, was to be preferred to its continued existence. Christ, on the other hand, opposed to the optimism of domination the optimism of redemption. Like Buddha, he saw evil in oppression, not in disobedience; whilst, in the imagination of other nations, the good gods had fought for the conquerors and the bad ones for the subjugated, he now represented the Jewish Jehovah as the Father of the poor and Satan as the idol of those who were in power. To him also the world was bad, but--and this was the decisive difference between him and Buddha--not radically so, but only because of the temporary sway of the devil. It was necessary, not to destroy the world, but to deliver it from the power of the devil, and therefore, in contrast to Buddhistic Quietism, he rightly called his church a 'militant' one. Both founders, however, being ignorant of the law of natural evolution, were at one in regarding the contemporary condition of civilisation as a permanent one, and therefore they agreed that oppression could be removed only by condemning riches and declaring poverty to be the only sinless state of man. The Indian king's son, familiar with all the wisdom of the Indians of his day, saw that reversion to universal poverty meant deterioration, therefore destruction, and, in his sympathy with the oppressed in their sorrow, he did not shrink from even this. The carpenter's Son from Galilee held the equality of poverty to be possible, and He was therefore far removed from the despondent resignation of His Indian predecessor--He proclaimed the optimism of poverty.

The later official Christianity has nothing at all in common with this teaching of Christ. The official Christianity is the outcome of the conviction, derived from experience, that the millennial kingdom of the poor preached by Christ and the Apostles is an impossibility, and of the consequent strange amalgamation of practical optimism with theoretical pessimism. Jehovah now again became the gaoler of the powerful, Satan the tempter who incites to disobedience to the commands of God; at the same time, however, the order of the world--though instituted by God--was declared to be fundamentally bad and incapable of improvement, the work of redemption no longer being regarded as referring to this world, but merely to the next. The exploiting world for the last fifteen centuries has naturally adhered to the new doctrine, leaving asceticism to a few anchorites and eccentric persons, whose conduct has remained without influence upon the sphere of practical human thought. Not until the last century, when the old industrial system approached its end, and the incipient control of man over nature gradually made the institution of servitude a curse to the higher classes, did pessimism--this time, philosophic pessimism--lift up its head once more. The world became more and more unpleasant even to the ruling classes; they were made to feel fettered and anxious by the misery around them, which they had previously been able easily to explain by a reference to the inscrutable counsels of God; they were seized by a dislike to those enjoyments which could be obtained only by the torture of their brethren, and, as they held this system, despite its horrible character, to be unchangeable, they gave themselves up to pessimism--the pessimism of Buddha, which looked for redemption only in the annihilation of just those more nobly constituted minds who did not allow themselves to be forced by the hereditary authoritative belief to mistake a curse for a blessing.

But another change is now about to be effected. The gods can no longer rule by terror over a race that has robbed the clouds of their lightning and the underworld of its fire; and, now that servitude has ceased to be the basis of the terrestrial order, it must also disappear from the celestial. The fear of God is as inconceivable as pessimism of any kind whatever as a characteristic of the coming generations, who, released from the suffering of the world, will pass their existence in the enjoyment of a lifelong happiness. For the great thinkers who, looking beyond their own times, give expression to truths the full meaning of which is understood only by subsequent generations, have never failed to see that this suffering, this 'original sin,' is based upon nothing else than the injustice of exploitation. The evils which mankind brought upon itself--want and vice--were what converted earth into hell; what nature imposed upon us--sickness and death--can no more embitter life to us than it can any other kind of living creatures. Sickness cannot, because it is only transitory and exceptional, especially since misery and vice no longer minister to it; and death cannot, because, in reality, it is not death, but merely the fear of it, which is an evil.

But it will be said that this fear of death, foolish as it may be in itself, is a real evil which is infinitely more painful to man, who reflects upon the future, than to the animal that lives merely in the present and knows of and fears death only when it is imminent. This was, in fact, the case, but it will not continue to be so when man, by his return to the innocence of nature, has won back his right to the painlessness of death. The fear of death is only one of the many specific instincts by which nature secures the perpetuation of species. If the beasts did not fear destruction, they would necessarily all perish, for their means of warding off the powerful dangers with which they are threatened are but weak. It is different with man, who has not merely become king of the living world, but has at last made himself master of the elements. In order to preserve the human species from perishing, nature needed to give to man the blind fear of death only so long as he had to defend himself against himself and his fellow-men. So long as he was the victim of the torture of subjection, man had also to think of death with emotions of invincible shuddering if he would not prefer destruction to suffering. Just because it was so painful, life had to be fenced round with the blind dread of death even in the case of that highest species, man, which did not need protection from external dangers. But now is this last and worst danger overcome; the dread of death has become superfluous even as a protection against suicide; it has no longer any use as a specific instinct of man, and it will disappear like every specific character which has become useless. This evil, also, will vanish with injustice from mankind; life spreads out full of serene joyousness before our successors, who, free from the crippling influence of pessimism, will spend their days in unending progress towards perfection.

But we, my friends, now hasten to open the doors to this future!

Here closed the sixth and last day of the Universal Congress of Eden Vale.

CONCLUSION

The history of 'Freeland' is ended. I could go on with the thread of the narrative, and depict the work of human emancipation as it appears to my mental eye, but of what use would it be? Those who have not been convinced, by what I have already written, that we are standing on the threshold of a new and happier age, and that it depends solely upon our discernment and resolve whether we pass over it, would not be convinced by a dozen volumes.

For this book is not the idle creation of an uncontrolled imagination, but the outcome of earnest, sober reflection, and of profound scientific investigation. All that I have described as really happening *might* happen if men were found who, convinced as I am of the untenability of existing conditions, determined to act instead of merely complaining. Thoughtlessness and inaction are, in truth, at present the only props of the existing economic and social order. What was formerly necessary, and therefore inevitable, has become injurious and superfluous; there is no longer anything to compel us to endure the misery of an obsolete system; there is nothing but our own folly to prevent us from enjoying that happiness and abundance which the existing means of civilisation are capable of providing for us.

It will perhaps be objected, 'Thus have numberless reformers spoken and written, since the days of Sir Thomas More; and what has been proposed to mankind as a panacea for all suffering has always proved to be Utopian.' And I am willing to admit that the dread of being classed with the legion of authors of Utopian romances at first filled my mind with not a few qualms as to the form which I had chosen for my book. But, upon mature deliberation, I decided to offer, not a number of dry abstractions, but as vivid a picture as possible, which should clearly represent in concrete conceptions what abstract ideas would have shown in merely shadowy outlines. The reader who does not for himself discover the difference between this book and the works of imagination above referred to, is lost to me; to him I should remain the 'unpractical enthusiast' even if I were to elaborate ever so dry a systematic treatise, for it is enough for him to know that I believe in a change of the existing system to condemn me as an enthusiast. It matters not, to this kind of readers, in what form I state my proofs; for such readers, like fanatics in the domain of religion, are simply disqualified to estimate aright the evidence which is pointed against what exists.

The impartial reader, on the other hand, will not be prevented by the narrative form of this book from soberly endeavouring to discover whether my propositions are essentially true or false. If he should find that I have started from false premises, that the system of freedom and justice which I have propounded is inconsistent in any way with the natural and universally recognised springs of human action--nay, if, after reading my book, he should not have attained to the firm conviction that the realisation of this new order--apart, of course, from unimportant details--is absolutely inevitable, then I must be content to be placed in the same category as More, Fourier, Cabet, and the rest who have mistaken their desires for sober reality.

I wish once more expressly to state that the intrinsic practicability of my book extends beyond the economic and ethical principles and motives underlying it, to the actual stage upon which its scenes are placed. The highlands in Equatorial Africa exactly correspond to the picture drawn in the book. In order that 'Freeland' may be realised as I have drawn it, nothing more is required, therefore, than a sufficient number of vigorous men. Shall I be privileged to live until these men are found?